Kissing Stars Over the Rising Sun

Paige Etheridge

ALL RIGHTS RESERVED

Publisher's Note:

This is a work of fiction. All names, characters, places, and events are the work of the author's imagination.

Any resemblance to real persons, places, or events is coincidental.

Solstice Publishing - www.solsticepublishing.com

"We are all born sexual creatures, thank God, but it's a pity so many people despise and crush this natural gift."
-Marilyn Monroe

For Sarah Caputo.

Every Sassafras will whisper your name. Every Lotus will
bloom in your memory.

Amaterasu created the universe as she saw fit. Every star, land, and sea belonged to her. She created the world and within it her land of the rising sun. The people there were to worship her and obey her laws.

In time, the Emperors and men of Japan seemed to forget they were descendants of the sun goddess. Though they still showed loyalty to their sun, their flag, they only served their own kind of men. They determined the level of worthiness of everyone else, forgetting Amaterasu created a whole universe beyond them.

War ensued.

Until another land, the land of the stars, won out, sending a deadly force of light. Their flag showed no daylight, but speckles in darkness. Cold and far away.

Night with no end fell over Japan for the first time since Amaterasu hid in a cave and left her world in darkness long ago. The sun was gone.

Through darkness, they emerged, the women of the night. Long repressed by the will and folly of their men, they cried out like wild animals and behaved as such. Free at last, they looked to feast as nocturnal creatures do. They craved the pleasures of the flesh. The men who brought them the night, the Americans, were the source of their pleasures. Their freedom.

Horrified at such a display, the Japanese men looked to extinguish these women. Politics, law, and Feminism became their allies against their common enemy. This was a war they wouldn't lose. The women disappeared into the shadows.

But these women echoed through the night. Their stories continued to live in the darkness, among the moon and stars. Until they were once again ready to emerge, show their place in the story of the land of the rising sun.

For the sun is also a star in a sea of eternal night. As is Amaterasu.

1945

Her country still seemed beautiful when she looked at Mount Fuji through the train window. Despite everything, war, pain, despair, and death, Japan's mighty mountain continued to rise as it always had. It loomed over the country's leaders whose intense desires to triumph pushed the Japanese soldiers to commit monstrosities. Life drained out of the country and extinction seemed inevitable. People died in insurmountable ways: through sacrificial plane crashes, starvation, disease, being torn apart by guns. The Japanese couldn't compete with their enemies this time, so they chose death. To kill and be killed. To keep the war going as long as one Japanese soldier stood. Signing death warrants for anyone who stood against them as well as their countrymen.

But before they could destroy themselves, they were overcome by a more powerful force. Americans. They had another plan. One that would lead to the surrender of people who believed in victory or death. Bombs. Miyako only heard rumors about them. The flashes of light which returned cities to the earth and left melted humans among the dust. Helpless creatures no one could rescue even if someone saw humanity left inside. People were too scared of how humans looked underneath despair and death. Ghosts roaming among the dead.

Japan lost the war. Failing to move ahead in the world despite having violently conquered its neighbors many times before. Bound into submission by a country whose power they longed to emulate, but couldn't repeat. In this hour of embarrassment and anguish, Japan awaited to be punished by the Americans insurmountable will.

When it was all over, many of the men left alive committed suicide in attempts to regain some reminisce of dignity. This angered Miyako. The age of the Samurai ended long ago, and such tactics achieved nothing. Honor killed more than it ever saved. At least, the kind of honor the Japanese cared about. She did not yet know how the Americans felt or perceived honor. She hoped their philosophy was better. Her life depended on it now, and she was scared. She was in the hands of a more powerful, deadly force.

Americans were coming in droves now. Conquerors now owned Japan. What would happen next, no one knew for certain. Fear lingered like the aroma of a recently burned forest. It invaded every part of her country, making everyone aware of their lost appetites for living, while still deciding whether to live or die.

If the Americans were willing to commit such horrors on those who never aimed a gun at them, what would they do to rest of the Japanese?

Yet, there the mountain stood as always, softly curving to the heavens, despite the sharp edges of this new existence. This great unknown put on her land. It was as if the mountain's presence was a sign not much had changed. But it had.

Miyako wondered if the mountain was dormant, asleep to the problems of the outside world. Or if it was wide awake, ready to burst into fiery flame as it had hundreds of years ago. Japan could still destroy itself after all. Did it matter?

Maybe the spirits would finally look down from the mountain to smile upon the Japanese people and aid them in this hour of need. Miyako gazed up at the snowy peak as the train pulled her closer alongside it. They certainly knew it was time, and would surely come to the rescue.

Reality clawed its way back to her heart and squeezed.

No. The spirits hadn't helped and still, they would not. Perhaps they weren't even real, or people didn't understand what they really were. Maybe their motivations were entirely different, the idea of helping humanity, pitiful and stupid. They could easily be neutral to human plights or had evil intent against mankind. Perhaps they wanted the Americans to come. People couldn't know the motives of such beings. Perhaps people prayed to the wrong spirits. Prayers delivered to the wrong beings wouldn't save anyone. But how could they know where to send them? They needed something they could easily know. Beings that would show themselves in order to be known. Feeling a presence was not enough. Believing, even less so. A person's mind was too fickle.

Such beings might not exist at all.

***

Miyako didn't want to end her life. Despite what terrors might be awaiting her, she wanted to believe something else was still possible. She didn't fear death, but anticipated welcoming it soon. She just wanted the chance to experience something else. She wanted to feel life before she lost it. No longer bound by the expectations placed upon her by culture, country, men, or women. In losing the war, Japan also lost its hold over her. By searching for some other kind of experience outside of all that, even if only for a moment, Miyako could finally experience life. Even for a fleeting moment.

That's why she left what remained of her fractured family behind. Her mother and sister cried day and night, waiting for death to silence them. She wouldn't let death find her among them: the family who didn't love her. Doctrine claimed her ancestors would never forgive her for what she'd done. She knew for sure her family wouldn't. They felt she owed them her death alongside them. Even without their love. But perhaps none of this truly mattered.

War changed everything by revealing the naked truth. Japan, her family, her faith, her history: none of those things were strong enough to hold in the face of war.

But she hadn't fallen in the face of war. Miyako was strong enough to remain standing. She sought to be rewarded for this. She wanted life in return.

She secretly packed her things and vanished into the night. Darkness hid her in its warm embrace. The light of the moon showed her just enough to reveal the way to the train. She waited at the station for hours in the dark. Miyako feared the spirits or her ancestors would come to devour her. Perhaps a stranger would kill her only to disappear into black anonymity. Or worse, her family would drag her back to their hell of tears and wails. She preferred any of the other scenarios to that one.

Dawn arrived, nothing else came for her. The light brought with it clarity that no one was coming to stop her. Miyako was free to go. She was grateful the night sheltered her. Protected her from her fears. Mother told her night was an enemy to all women. Night was her ally. She would turn to it for the rest of her life.

What else was mother wrong about?

Miyako got on the first train that eagerly took her, despite its wear and tear. As the train pushed her forward, and she paid her fare, there was no turning back. She didn't have enough money to return. Everyone was too poor to spare her anything that could bring her home. The funds she'd stolen to escape could have been used to pay for a few meals for her family, but it wasn't enough to save them. It was money she used to take herself elsewhere. It was never theirs. She owed them nothing. War changes everything. Proving undeserved loyalty should be paid back in kind.

Her dishonor toward her family was complete as she sat down in her seat and got comfortable. As punishment, her ancestors and other spirits would be coming for her soon, according to what she'd been taught. Yet, there was no need to care about any of this. She was already being punished for a war and a defeat she wasn't responsible for. Neither her ancestors nor the spirits helped her family or her country. When the lights of hope went out, no one came to save them. Her father and brothers promised to win the war. Instead, they died, leaving behind women without any means to care for themselves. Her family vowed to take care of her and each other despite this. They failed too.

Miyako would serve herself instead. What mattered now was her own survival, whether she lived for a few more terrifying days or languished through years of loneliness. She sought her prize, the other side of the war. Even a few idle moments of joy would be worth it for her, however transient. All beautiful things were. Just like the cherry blossoms, she loved so much.

***

Tokyo looked different than Miyako imagined it would. She somehow maintained the slightest hope that the devastation of the war didn't hit Tokyo. That the Tokyo she'd heard about long ago would embrace her with an existence of normalcy. Looking through the window, she saw this wasn't the case. The past was gone. Every part of Japan was forced into this painful present. The broken-souled people were here too. Their eyes told the story they shared as their personal failures and sorrows were kept hidden.

Miyako stood scared on the platform after she got off the train. She couldn't lose herself in the crowd surrounding her, because she didn't want to be among these people. She waited there for a while. No one touched her, not even an accidental bump, as if they knew she wasn't one of them. The war affected her. Miyako was on the other side of it now. What that meant, she wasn't sure. The war affected everyone, but felt it moved her in a completely different way. Perhaps it was because she'd also been affected by the night.

She felt more alone than ever. She prayed to no one and anyone to help her silently in her head, to help her survive.

That's when she heard strange laughter.

Miyako looked across the station to see an oddly dressed Japanese woman getting cozy with a pair of American GIs. One of the men ran his hands over her while the other watched by their side. Miyako was in awe of the mysterious woman's boldness. Japan hadn't censored her at all.

The woman wore a black dress that fit tightly around her body. Her stomach was tight and led to round childbearing hips. Her legs were long and graceful, like a crane standing in a river. Miyako could see her voluptuous breasts and even her nipples with the distance between them. Miyako wondered what it would feel like for a man to run his hands across such a body. Miyako was glad no one saw her blush at her thoughts. Even though the thought itself brought her such shame, she found herself wishing a man would run his hands across her own body in such a manner.

To avoid the tingle in her groin, Miyako examined other parts of the woman and avoided looking at the two men entirely. Her hair was curly and shiny. Her hair seemed to have a life of its own, despite its stillness. On top of her head was a pair of glasses, but the lenses were dark. Miyako had never saw a pair like that before. She wore black shoes that brought her heels higher than her toes. Her nails and lips were bright red and contrasted with her skin beautifully like a Fuji apple. She was leaning against a wall chewing with an open mouth on something pink.

The man who was touching her moved his arms around her waist and leaned in to kiss her. But it wasn't a short peck as Miyako expected. The kissing continued for a long time with movements from both their mouths and yet a certain stillness about it all. Miyako had never seen this before. This wasn't allowed in her old Japan. But it was present in the new one. She wondered what it felt like. She hadn't known people could kiss like that.

When they finished kissing, the woman started laughing as the man moved his mouth over her neck. She was loud and smiling with all her teeth. She was having the time of her life. At least, that's how it looked to Miyako. Miyako eyed the woman's beauty and confidence, how her body's curves were as white as an early snowfall like Yuki-Onni. Perhaps that's why she wielded such power; those fox spirits were irresistible to the lovers they chose.

It was clear she was sleeping with the enemy. A traitor to her own people. A mockery of everything the Japanese stood for, and everything the people been through. Miyako should hate her, as she was sure the rest of Japan did. Yet, she envied her.

Everyone was looking at that woman. She was the center of her own show. She wasn't acting like a proper Japanese woman. Miyako longed to be her even though she felt this was a terrible thought. As if hearing her thoughts, the woman turned to look at Miyako.

Her eyes were dark and mischievous like the fox spirit Miyako suspected her to be. They burned right into Miyako. Painful to Miyako's eyes.

Miyako looked down in embarrassment before quietly sneaking into the station's dark bathroom. She still was getting her bearings for where she was. She needed to shake off that look. She hid in a stall as she sat to pee. She hadn't thought about what she was going to do when she made it to Tokyo. Part of her hadn't thought she'd get this far.

Instinct told her those fox eyes would find her. Perhaps even prey upon her. Be her end. She never thought women could be dangerous before.

The bathroom door opened with a rusty sigh followed by the clicking of high heels. Those fox eyes coming near her. The woman she'd seen outside entered the bathroom. Miyako scooted forward to watch through a crack in the door as she walked in and headed to the sink.

She took off her big black glasses and leaned toward the mirror, a short line away from where Miyako sat. Miyako observed how this woman's facial features were sharp. She was the most Japanese-like person she'd seen in a long time, if ever. She hadn't turned into a ghost like the others, and she'd kept a handle on herself despite the war. The woman clenched her teeth and used her red nails to pick at her teeth. Her presence hypnotized Miyako. Then her voice echoed through the room.

"How long are you going to stare at me from there?" The woman said. The sound of her voice was similar to audio knives being driven into Miyako's ears. The noise shocked her and hurt.

"Come here," the woman said. She still maintained the volume but kept the hostile edge out of her voice. She looked at Miyako through the mirror.

Miyako couldn't move. She was locked in the woman's gaze like a spider in a web.

"You're shy I see. That's not going to work." The woman turned and walked toward Miyako's stall. She opened it and stared down at Miyako. Her eyes shone like diamonds in the darkness. Quickly her eyes were drawn to Miyako's heated crotch, which was still open from peeing just moments before. Not in a way of yearning, but of knowing. A slow smile crept across her face as her eyes lingered there. Miyako's fear kept her still, even with her legs still open.

"Still, you might fit this line of work after all. You speak English?"

"Yes, I was training at Gion before…"

Shinju turned away and walked back to the sink, not caring to hear any more. Miyako stopped her line of dialogue. The woman returned her gaze to Miyako.

"Good enough. Come here. I'm Shinju."

Shinju used English when she spoke, not Japanese. In fact, she hadn't spoken a word of Japanese. Miyako felt that was the only language the woman found acceptable. She'd respond as such.

Slowly, Miyako got up and walked over to her, nearly forgetting to hide her sex under her clothes once more. Miyako stopped just behind her, still feeling herself in that strange trance state. Pulled into a beautiful web. She feared the woman, yet couldn't dare tear herself away from her. She had her now. Shinju turned back toward the mirror and started rummaging through her bag.

"You got any money?"

"Very little. I spent most of it on the train here."

"Why did you come here?"

"I'd hope to find work," Miyako was surprised by her own response. There never was a plan.

"Doing what?"

"I don't know."

"Figures." Miyako felt the vibration of her tone pierce through her throat, chest, and crotch. The woman continued to move through her purse.

Shinju pulled out a fat stack of green rectangular paper. American money. It was more money than Miyako ever seen in her life. Shinju used both her hands to build a pile with all the bills. She took her left hand and lifted them to her mouth. She kissed them long but gently. Shinju put all the bills away but one and left her bag open.

"Do you want money?"

"Oh no, I couldn't take any."

Shinju's eyes darkened, "Not mine. Your own."

"I'm not sure if I understand." Miyako turned to Shinju as moved the last bill off the table and slid it into her hand. Her eyes showed an intensity that had Miyako's knees shaking. Those weren't the eyes of a human being. Their bottomless darkness held the mysteries humans spent their whole lives a part of, but not understanding. It was the same darkness that sheltered her in the night. Maybe this woman was one of those allusive Kitsune, seducing people to their bidding. Or perhaps, she was a merely a being who belonged to the night. Miyako was free to go along for the ride.

Shinju started to pull different things out of her bag with the hand not touching the paper bill.

"What's that?" asked Miyako.

"Makeup. You've never worn any?"

"I have, but not like that."

Shinju turned to look at Miyako, forcing her to lower her eyes. It was as if she needed to shield her eyes from an overly bright moon.

"I'll teach you everything you need to know. If you want this."

"Want what?"

"The money." Shinju waved the bill in front of Miyako. She brought it close enough to Miyako's face, so the green paper barely touched her lips. Then in a circular motion, Shinju skimmed those green tips over Miyako's breasts and nipples. Miyako held stilled.

Shinju brought the bill back to her own lips and kissed the man's face.

Shinju continued as she examined Miyako's body, "The chance to take back from the Americans all we lost in the war and more. The Japanese men have nothing for us. But the Americans have plenty. Let's beat the men at their own power game. Let's take from them what's we've been denied through their lust for power over everything, including us." Her eyes rose back to Miyako's, "You're certainly pretty enough for it. A beautiful woman has a lot of sway over a man."

"I'm not understanding," Miyako lied. She understood perfectly.

"I know you're not that dumb," Shinju retorted.

"But sleeping with the enemy?"

"What other choice do you have?" She positioned the bill in front of Miyako's lips again. "What pride for your country do you have left? America owns us now. What else are we good for?"

Miyako retreated into her mind. Was she prepared to betray her country? She didn't owe her country or her family anything. She never had. They had left her without any skill, money, or means to support herself. Her people, especially her men failed her. She wouldn't be here with Shinju otherwise.

This was her chance to survive. Perhaps even find some elusive joys along the way.

Truthfully, the idea of being with Americans gave Miyako a tingle. She'd often dreamed of being with powerful warriors. Ones of a foreign land with strong bodies, sharp minds, tales of adventure, and a touch of mystery. She'd never told anyone this. It would have been shameful to admit such fantasies of romances with foreign men. Her own stories kept her up at night. The only time she was free to dream of such things. Alone in the dark.

Secretly she never found Japanese men attractive.

Now, she would have a chance to fill her hunger for the exotic. To explore the side she'd hidden away for so long. Learn the experiences of romance, love. Leave the world satisfied, in a mutual fashion.

No one knew her in Tokyo. All the judgment would be from complete strangers. This was the best payback she could ever think of.

She could always leave if she wanted to, right? This was her choice. She chose whether to live or die each day. She could make up what was left of her life now. At least it would be hers to the end. Her family couldn't stop her or control her anymore. Instead of paying for other people's mistakes, at last now she'd only be paying for her own.

"So what do you say?" Shinju asked again.

Miyako kissed the man on the bill gingerly, then smiled. Shinju grinned in turn.

"Good girl," Shinju grabbed Miyako's hand and slipped the bill into Miyako's palm and closed her hand around it. She then used both her hands to move the hair away from Miyako's face. "Consider that a small advance. What's your name?"

"Miyako."

Shinju smiled again but broader this time, "Beautiful. Night. Child. City. Perfect."

Shinju turned her attention back to the makeup near the sink before focusing again on Miyako, "You're pretty right now. But that won't be enough for any of these men. Let's make you look hot."

"Hot?"

"It's an American thing. I'll teach you what you need to know. Stay still." Shinju picked up a short and fat stick and pulled off a piece to reveal something red and shiny inside, like a jewel. She held Miyako's face with a talon grip and put it to her mouth.

"We have to do these touch-ups quick," said Shinju as she placed the red tipped stick back on the counter and stared at Miyako's now red lips, "The men are waiting."

Miyako took a breath as Shinju picked up a brush with rosy powder and began to paint her face. She stood there, her breaths short and shallow. Shinju stopped to recheck her work only to switch to another brush and powder, which was darker, ordering Miyako to close her eyes.

"What are the Americans like?" Miyako asked.

"They're nice enough to give us business because they're horny," said Shinju. "They have lots of money for the two of us. Tons of presents too. It'll be like Christmas every day! They're all like Santa Claus. But sexier and not fat."

"What's Christmas? Is Santa Claus an American movie star?"

Shinju chuckled. "I'll let one of the Americans explain it to you." She moved on to painting Miyako's eyes, "We're going to need to curl your hair and buy some new clothes. You'll need to look more American to get clients. For now, this will be enough."

***

During the date, Miyako stayed quiet while everyone else did the talking. She'd never had burgers, fries, and soda before. It was the biggest meal she'd seen in years. She devoured and savored every bite.

"Wow, you were starving!" one of the men said.

Miyako simply smiled and nodded in turn.

"I like a girl with a good appetite. Here." He wiped Miyako's face with a napkin. She loved the smell of his hand wafting under her nose. A mix of musk and earth.

For Miyako, this was the first taste of cherry cola, shyness caused names to be forgotten, sunglasses were defined, whipped cream on the nose proving to be a flirty gesture, and quick kisses good-bye came all too soon.

The men paid for everything and left the women money. Shinju split the amount in half with Miyako.

"Is that really it? That's all we had to do?"

Shinju nodded.

"Sometimes it will be like that," she said. "There are days men just want to share a meal or watch a movie. Other times they'll just want sex. Usually, they'll want both. Like the clients who we're meeting with tonight. They're expecting both."

"Why is that?"

"Sometimes men want a girlfriend, and sometimes they want sex. A girlfriend still gives sex though, but they also make men less lonely. We're their substitutes while they're stuck here with us."

"How do you have sex?"

Shinju snickered. "You really don't know?"

Miyako shook her head.

Shinju sighed, "That's the benefits of the Americans at least. They'll teach you everything you need to know. However," Shinju smiled at Miyako. "I'll get you started."

"We're practicing the art of romance?"

Shinju laughed, "Sure. Whatever. Call it what you will. I call it fucking."

***

Shinju lead Miyako back to her apartment. Miyako was so amazed that Shinju had her own place, she ignored the whirlwind of American clothes and magazines all in English, littering every conceivable space, except the bed. The bed laid there white and naked, in wait of occupants of any kind. Sweat and a powdery perfume hung heavily in the air.

There were no Shōjis, sliding doors with translucent paper to let in the light. No place for a pot or to store rice. Calligraphy didn't have a place here. There were no mats or bamboo. No kimonos or lingering aromas of past cooking over a fire. Shoes weren't isolated and placed outside the home, they were scattered all over the floor.

This wasn't a Japanese home. This was a home in another world.

Miyako hoped she could attain the same.

Shinju told Miyako to take off her clothes. Miyako stripped and handed her clothes to Shinju's outreached hands. These were the only possessions Miyako brought with her on the train.

Shinju tore them apart.

Miyako smiled, delighted as she watched the destruction. Miyako covered as much of her own nakedness as she could with her hands. Shinju ripped the clothing into smaller shreds, letting them fall into a pile. She used a piece to wipe off her lipstick, another to wipe Miyako's lips clean. Shinju took the pile she'd made and threw it into the corner of the room furthest away from Miyako.

Miyako watched and waited for Shinju to offer direction on what to do next. She assumed Shinju would provide a change of clothes. But Shinju didn't. She told Miyako to lie down on the bed. Miyako did as she was told, keeping as much of her nakedness hidden from Shinju as possible. She put her head on the pillow and turned her eyes to the bare ceiling. The smell of Shinju, and her lovers lingered in the sheets.

"I'm only going to go over this with you once, so pay attention," Shinju said as she moved Miyako's hands off her personal areas, placing them on either side of her stomach. "I need to teach you a few things, so you don't make a complete fool of me with my clients. So you don't make a fool of yourself and end up with no lovers."

Shinju approached Miyako and positioned her body over hers on the bed. Shinju would be playing the role of a man. A man Miyako would need to please.

Miyako lifted her head to speak. To ask what would happen. But she was unable to complete her question because Shinju's lips mirrored hers, silencing any hesitations or objections. Leaving only the sounds of their mouths opening and closing to each other.

Did women touch each other like this out of pleasure or love? Or was it only to prepare for making love to a man? Would one of them remain clothed, as Shinju was? Even her sunglasses were still above her head.

Heat and moisture ran into Miyako loins. Her breathing struggled to keep up with her heart rate through the taste of smoke and residual lipstick. Shinju didn't seem to take in enough air before falling into Miyako again. It was as if she didn't need to breathe at all, or she'd found a way to do so through Miyako.

Shinju ran her hands over Miyako's chest, cupping her breasts. Shinju gently pushed them to form higher mountains then smoothed them into shorter hills only to repeat the rhythm. Adding and releasing pressure, only to squeeze them even harder.

Miyako felt fire coursing through her, a river of heat in an icy world.

Shinju rubbed her fingers on Miyako's nipples. Shinju gingerly kissed Miyako's breast before sucking on her nipples occasionally nipping Miyako's breast with her teeth. Miyako did her best not make any noise though each act committed upon her made it harder not to. She, instead, watched Shinju and took mental notes. Lessons to becoming a romantic expert for the Americans.

When Shinju finished with her breast, she moved her hands over Miyako's whole body except for the part of her that bloomed open, pink, and delicate. The sensations Miyako felt were alien to her but touched upon some primal need deep inside of her, one she thought she must have inherited from thousands of generations ago.

Shinju looked at Miyako's groin and moved her fingers along the top of it. Miyako couldn't help but groan. Shinju continued to run her hands over the flesh, first slowly, then gradually more intensely, until it was as if a petal was skating over a lake.

"Open your legs more," Shinju ordered Miyako. "You'll need them open for the men to have their way with you. Let me see into you."

Miyako spread her legs apart.

Shinju thrust her fingers up into Miyako's vaginal tunnel, and she jolted. Shinju stared her down.

"What's going inside you is going to be a lot bigger than my fingers. American cocks are huge. Thick and long. Not like the Japanese ones at all. They feel better too," Shinju said. "Relax, so you'll be able to let all of it in. It will feel better for you, too. You'll be able to experience fully all the American cock has to offer."

Shinju moved her fingers up and down inside of Miyako. "They're going to move up and down inside of you like this," she said.

Miyako was still until Shinju grabbed her hip with her free hand and coaxed Miyako into a circular motion.

"Men don't want you to hold still like a dead fish," Shinju said. "They want you to move with them. They want to believe you're enjoying their hands on you, their lips with yours, and their cocks inside you. It gets them off. Move your hips in rhythm with my movements. Up and down along my hand. You'll do this with their dicks inside of you."

The movements felt awkward to Miyako at first. Shinju looked at her several times in frustration. Miyako refused to fail. Aside from this, she wanted to prove to herself she could please a man. Soon, Miyako was moving correctly, she could tell through the feelings in her vagina and through the changes in Shinju's face who appeared pleased. Shinju released Miyako from her grasp. Miyako sighed in relief. She was past Shinju's test.

Moments later, Shinju's mouth was on her vagina. Miyako giggled.

Shinju looked up at Miyako in frustration again, "You are not to laugh when a man does this to you," she said. "I am going to continue until I know you won't laugh at them."

"I'm sorry," Miyako said. There was more to sex than Miyako could have ever imagined.

Shinju slapped her. "I told you not to talk. Do you know how weird it is to be touching a woman like this? I'm doing this as a big favor to you. I don't need to do this. I could find another girl who already knows how to fuck. Be grateful I'm teaching you so you can make money from the Americans. Now stay on your back until I tell you I'm finished. No laughing or making any dumb noises. You're only getting one lesson from me."

Miyako nodded. Shinju returned her mouth to Miyako's lower region but hovered above it to finish her thought.

"Make a lot of noise though," Shinju said. "They like that. It makes them feel good about what they're doing to us. Don't be silent. It creeps them out. Just don't scream unless they're fucking you really hard."

Shinju's lips and tongue landed on Miyako's bloomed parts again. Shinju's tongue was soft yet aggressive as she worked to show her what to expect. Miyako moaned, exhaling loudly, happy to be releasing at least some of the tension building in her body, from years of denying this part of herself. The sexual yearning always shoved into the darkness, hidden but never forgotten. Leaving in its wake, hunger and pain. She moved her hips the way she had when Shinju's fingers were inside of her.

"Much better," Shinju said as she wiped her mouth. "You're acting like a real lover now." Shinju shoved her fingers up Miyako's ass. Miyako yelped.

"Yes, I know, but some men really like it," Shinju said. "Move your hips like you were before."

Miyako did. Did men really put their dicks there? How many men would do this to her? It was even tighter than her vagina! How would she ever handle an American penis? Actually, Miyako wondered what a dick looked like. She thought of all the ways a dick could look to avoid thinking about Shinju's fingers up her ass. Like a snake or eel. Root or branch. Pen or finger. She hoped they were well designed for sexual activities. Soft enough to not hurt her, but hard enough to drive her wild.

"Very good," Shinju said. "You may still be a virgin, but you're fuckable now at least. Your virginity will be gone by tonight. Now there's another position men like. Kneel on the bed."

Miyako rose for the first time since they started. She came forward with her knees as Shinju asked and bent over as she command. Shinju used her hands to show Miyako where to lower her back and raise her butt.

"Men will put their dicks in you from here into both holes," she said. "This applies to other positions as well. Now if their dick goes in here." Shinju put her finger back into Miyako's ass, and she yelped again. "Make sure they don't put it into your mouth or pussy after that. You could get sick, or make other clients sick. That's bad for business. Tell them they have to finish in your ass or wash up and watch them if necessary. A horny man is reliable only for his business with you. You must ensure you remain in working condition for everyone else."

Shinju kept her finger in Miyako's ass and used her other hand to move Miyako forward and back, telling her to use her knees to create the movement.

"There are many more positions, but these should be enough for now."

Shinju spanked her.

Miyako screamed.

"This isn't a punishment. American men like doing this. It turns them on. Let them do it." Shinju rubbed Miyako's butt over the spot she'd hit, only to smack it again. She hit the other cheek twice before letting Miyako sit back down on the bed.

"We're going to practice kissing again," Shinju said. "Remember to move with me. They don't want to fuck a dead body. Be submissive but not dead. They want a hot breathing sexy woman to stick their cocks in."

They saw enough dead bodies in the war, Miyako thought to herself.

Miyako remained naked as she kissed Shinju, who still never so much as removed the sunglasses on top of her head. They kissed into the night. When the darkness was complete, and all the light was gone, Shinju finally stopped.

"Good girl," Shinju said, kissing Miyako's forehead. "Now you're old life is behind you. Sex is your new future. Let's find you something to wear. As much as the men would love it, you can't go out naked. They need to pay for the merchandise."

Shinju walked to her closet. Without turning to Miyako, who was leaving the bed, she added, "We're never doing that again. You understand? You are to tell no one."

Miyako nodded. Shinju didn't look at her to see her response.

Shinju presented Miyako with a cream-colored dress patterned with vibrant flowers. Miyako asked what kind of flowers they were, and Shinju told her it didn't matter. Miyako told herself they were roses. She would be like an American rose, she thought to herself.

Miyako moved her hands on the dress, feeling the fabric in her fingers. Silky like petals in water. She slipped into the dress and loved the sensation on the rest of her body. She hugged back the dress, which was embracing her. This is how she would dress from now on.

"I'm sexy like a movie star. You're just a little sexy right now. That's why this will look good on you," Shinju said, rummaging through the mountains of clothes in her closet, finding a pair of bright red high-heeled shoes that matched the flowers on the dress "But sex will change you. You'll become completely sexy too. At least to the Americans. You'll find your own style in time."

Shinju seemed deep in thought and paused, but then continued.

"You'll be able to afford your own clothes and place soon. But for now, you'll stay with me and use my stuff. Only the clothes I give you though. I'll beat you if you wear anything without my permission. Most of these things are still only mine, and I plan to keep it that way. Here," Shinju said to Miyako as she handed her matching shoes.

Miyako slipped the shoes onto her feet. She felt so much taller now, but she was still shorter than Shinju.

"I need to do your makeup again," Shinju said touching Miyako's face. "But soon you're going to have to learn to do it by yourself. I won't touch your face again. Or anything else of yours."

Shinju told Miyako to sit on the bed again so she could complete her makeup. Miyako heard Shinju ramble with instructions involving the soldiers, but Miyako wasn't listening. Her mind was still catching up to where she was and what she was doing. Part of herself felt so far away.

***

When both women donned a fresh layer of colors on their faces as well as perfume on their wrist and necks, a method of use Miyako noted, they left the apartment. After walking a short distance, a few times in which Miyako almost tripped in her heels, but they arrived at a corner near a movie theatre and stopped to wait without actually doing so.

Miyako wondered what would come of this night. She was beyond sore from Shinju. Raw and heated. Miyako wanted to kiss a soldier like she had seen Shinju do earlier that day. Like she'd practiced with Shinju. She wondered how much differently a man's lips and tongue would feel compared to hers.

Shinju leaned on the wall behind her, and Miyako copied her. Miyako didn't like leaning up against the wall. It made her back itch. She observed how Shinju didn't seem to mind having her back against the building, while waiting outside the movie theater. She used the concrete to make herself taller. Miyako wondered why Shinju wasn't itchy from the wall. Miyako rubbed her back against the building hoping to find some nook where her back didn't feel like dragon claws were drawing across her skin. She considered just standing in front of the wall instead. She didn't have to do exactly everything like Shinju.

Shinju blew smoke into Miyako's face.

"You're moving too much," Shinju snorted. "Be a graceful woman, not a child."

Miyako took note. Using her heels as a kickstand, she leaned her shoulders, which still itched against the wall Her heels hurt a bit, but she enjoyed the tight feeling in her feet. A few minutes later, a GI whistled at her as he walked by. His eyes lingered on her legs.

"Don't take all the men away from me," Shinju retorted loudly. "But keep showing off your legs like that. It's going to bring us more customers."

Shinju blew a bubble with the pink shape she was chewing on.

"How do you do that?"

Shinju passed Miyako a piece from her purse.

"You put the gum over your tongue and then blow like this, not too hard." Shinju blew another bubble.

After a few tries, Miyako was seeing pink spheres forming from her own lips. Each one was unique, despite being formed from the same piece of gum. A few moments of artistic glory before joyfully bursting.

Shinju laughed when a bubble exploded before it finished launching from Miyako's mouth.

Miyako smiled back.

Yet, Miyako noticed Shinju seemed distant from her. She wouldn't look Miyako in the eye. Perhaps this too was part of her methods. To keep her sexual energy focused on the men. When a soldier passed by, Shinju's charms were at play. They seemed exaggerated from Miyako's closer view, almost to the point of embarrassing her. Her screams of a man's hotness, hard looks between their legs, or dramatic facial expressions to lure in a lover were expressed with heavy force. It surprised Miyako she wasn't exhausted from it. Yet, Shinju received outspoken masculine approval in return. Though none of these potentials proved fruitful.

Miyako was curious about what else could happen between two women as she watched Shinju's display. But she was more curious about being with men. The approval and fulfillment of men is what she truly longed for.

Two uniformed GIs approached, one of them had dark skin which reminded Miyako of the dark sky. Was this what a man of the night looked like? He was the one she desired. Miyako whistled at him.

She could see the moons in his eyes when he returned her eye contact. He was beautiful. He approached with the other man in tow.

Shinju nudged Miyako, "Good work."

***

After some talk in which Shinju asked for some gum, even though she had plenty of her own, the four were off for the night. Shinju partnered up with the creamy-skinned GI named Greg. Miyako was left with the dark one named Roger. Miyako did her best to disguise her delight in catching the man she wanted.

Miyako liked how Roger smelled. The musky aroma of a strong man without the telltale signs of a smoker. Greg only smelled of cigarettes. She could smell him even though he was arm and arm with Shinju. Even after they bought food and drinks at the concession stand and sat down to watch the movie, the smell was loud on the nostrils. How was Shinju not bothered by it?

"Why are you two together? I thought you guys didn't like each other." Shinju smacked her gum loudly as she turned her head toward her client. Greg turned to Roger who sat with Miyako in the row behind him.

Miyako giggled awkwardly, confused by Shinju's statement.

"What do you mean?" Greg said.

"You type of guys always seem to complain about black guys."

Miyako swallowed hard. Did she really just say that?

"Nah, we're beyond that. We grew up together. We're brothers. One day the world will realize that too."

Miyako exhaled in relief.

"You must have had one ugly momma for you two to look so different."

"No, Mom was a beautiful lady," Greg looked down and reached into his coat pocket.

"Was? Is she ugly now?"

"No, she died. Here." He took out a picture from his breast pocket and handed it to Shinju.

Shinju smiled broadly and kept chewing her gum, "She's pretty. Like a movie star."

"Yeah. Like a movie star. She always wanted to be in the movies."

Miyako turned to Roger, "What about you?"

"My mom died when I was born, so I never met her."

"How did she die?"

"Childbirth."

"What does it mean for two guys like you to be together?"

Shinju turned from her movie seat and hit Miyako.

"Don't ask questions like that!" Shinju was laughing.

"But you just…" Miyako started.

"It's fine," Roger added to finish Miyako's comment. "I guess this girl here hasn't seen the darker side of racism."

"The Japanese are the most racist of all," Miyako said darkly. She remembered hearing remarks about anyone from any of land being inferior. It was always said in such a horrible way. Miyako blocked most of it out. Yet, she couldn't imagine how such a beautiful man could be discriminated against in the same way. Were others simply jealous? Or stupid?

"Meanwhile, you guys can't tell the difference between the Koreans and us." Shinju sounded almost sad about it.

"I'm sorry. I shouldn't have asked," Miyako chimed. "What would you like to talk about?"

"You know anything about planes? I fly them," Roger said.

"Oh! Do you feel like a bird when you do that?"

Roger laughed. "This might sound corny, but I feel more like a comet when I do that. Like I could fly through the whole universe if I wanted to."

Miyako started laughing too, "That sounds great! I'd like to be a shooting star myself!"

Roger smiled.

The lights dimmed, and Shinju told Miyako to be quiet. The movie started.

It hit Miyako then. Much already was different from America and Japan. They brought delicious food. Their films showed a lot of kissing, which at first embarrassed then delighted Miyako. There were already new businesses catering to their desires. Miyako was just one more.

Miyako watched the screen pondering all of this as Roger inched his hand toward her knee. She turned around to look at Shinju who pushed to see this particular picture, to find her paying no attention to the screen as she furiously made out with Greg. Miyako grabbed some popcorn from

Shinju's bag and turned back around to watch the movie. She anticipated being touched again and feeling all of those wild things from such activity. She started shaking a bit.

"Do you want me to stop? I don't want to make you uncomfortable."

Miyako shook her head. Then, realizing her date might not see her in the dark she leaned to whisper in his ear as well.

"I'm fine. Just too much soda." Miyako was on her third serving of coke before she noticed it made her jittery and energetic. But she was mostly responding to nerves. She didn't want him to stop. He excited her too much for her not to react. At least with Shinju, she could mostly keep herself still. That wasn't happening with Roger.

Miyako wanted to feel what it was like to go all the way. This was the best she'd felt in her entire life. She loved being able to make these choices, all of which were deliciously forbidden. She was dictating this and Roger was giving her the opportunity to do so. She would let him put his penis in her. Considering he'd be her first, she felt joy and relief.

"You're so sweet," Miyako told Roger as she kissed him on the cheek. It was the first time she'd ever kissed a man, and her groin was on fire already. "I can't wait until we make love tonight."

Miyako saw Roger smile in the dark. He opted to hold her hand instead, stroking the top of it with his thumb. At first, she thought she might have turned him off. But she knew in her heart that he was saving everything for after the movie.

***

Yet in the deepening night, as they reached the hotel, Miyako's heart began to race. What if she didn't perform up to expectation? How could she compare to other lovers he'd been with, especially since he was paying her?

She was too embarrassed to admit to him she was inexperienced with lovemaking. Shinju's demonstrations on her showed just how much she didn't know when it came to the vast possibilities of lovemaking. There were so many things two bodies could do together! She hadn't even practiced on a man yet. Revealing any of this information wasn't going to make her any money. Worse case, she'd turn off Roger. Miyako wanted him to want her.

Would it be as easy as Shinju said? Shinju made it seem so complicated when she'd showed her what could be done. Maybe Shinju was just better at this kind of thing than Miyako. She didn't want to embarrass herself or Shinju.

Shinju showed her these things came naturally. There was a fluidity which occurred between two people when they made love if they were prepared to both bring themselves together. They would flow together like a river, sometimes smooth and gentle, other times hard and swift. They could find stillness too.

Miyako had to have faith Shinju taught her enough. But most importantly, confidence in herself would allow her to reach new heights of pleasure with someone else. With this man in particular.

Shinju was laughing with Greg as they hung over each other and headed toward their room. From down the hall, "Don't worry, black men are really nice," Shinju called out as Greg pulled her into their room.

The door slammed. Shinju and Greg were out of sight. The laughter was replaced with different noises coming from their room. But these sounds were muffled to the point that they didn't count for anything at all. Especially after she and Roger entered their own room and closed the door.

After she and Roger entered their room, Miyako moved to sit on the bed as he closed the door, unsure what to do next. She stayed still and didn't say anything for a few minutes as embarrassment rushed through her. How would she even start?

Roger started for her. Without saying a word, he leaned in and kissed her.

Heat exploded through her body. Especially in her lower region, which had already been building since she'd first set her eyes on Roger. Her tongue played with his. Hands found places and rhythms. Shinju's techniques proved useful. Miyako was amazed everything was coming together. Instinctively.

She knew then, despite what she'd been led to believe in her old life, such actions were inherently part of people. Then why was it, especially for women, such desires were locked away? It was all so natural. A need, which left unattended, would leave people to starve and die. These sexual drives were in everyone.

No matter what, she was happy she would be holding herself back no longer. She felt no more shame, no more embarrassment. She would express herself as she wanted to, right here in this bedroom and with every other man she encountered. She would get what she wanted from them, and in turn, they would get what they wanted from her. By serving them, she would be serving herself. She would finally be finding satisfaction. After all the years of hiding the same sexual yearning everyone contained, she'd get her fill. She felt fortune and luck was on her side for the first time. She'd been led to this, and she would return in turn with servitude and loyalty.

No wonder Shinju seemed to be having so much fun with this job.

Roger took the rest from there. As Shinju told her, he led the way, from beginning to end. He took off both their clothes, quickly but respectfully. Between kissing and caressing all her parts, he continually asked if she was okay to move forward. She nodded and kissed him each time. When he finally put his dick into her Miyako jolted not out of pain or surprise, but from at the shock of feeling truly alive. A shattering of something old within her to release something new. Breaking into and reaching her most soft parts, her womanhood. Loving the man who entered her there and who loved her femininity.

This was something she gave to him and only him, something special they shared. No other man would ever have this.

His penis felt better than a pair of sharply manicured fingers for sure. It still hurt some, but Miyako could tell it was just from her body adjusting to lovemaking. A penis was definitely designed to please a woman's insides. It massaged and filled her. The feeling of it moved through her whole body. A penis belonged in a vagina. It was at home there. Dicks floated along male bodies as they went about life and other activities that mostly had nothing to do with sex. But when a woman opened herself to a man, the penis could finally be itself, an erotic tool, and the pleasure was shared by the parties involved. Miyako was letting Roger come home in her. Miyako moaned, letting him know how happy this made her and kissed whatever muscles of his she could reach.

That night, an American taught her how to make love. She was freed.

***

The next day Miyako bled from her vagina. She only noticed after Roger left, and before Shinju knocked on the hotel door to check on her.

Shinju told Miyako it was normal for a first time. When Miyako asked if she would always bleed after sex, she replied.

"Only if you fuck like an animal. Come on. We need to clean up at my place and get some sleep before we come back out for the night. I'm hungry too. Do you want breakfast?"

Miyako nodded.

They repeated the same routine as the night before except at a bowling alley with different dates who could at least tell Miyako what bowling was.

The next night played out the same as the first. Despite different places and faces.

And the next.

***

Shinju almost always wore black. She told Miyako it made a woman look skinny and sexy. It gave a woman a certain sense of mystery, one that drew men in. Black turned men wild with passion, so much so that they had to rip off your clothes to see what's underneath.

Miyako hadn't seen women dress in all black before meeting Shinju. She wasn't sure if one ever had. It was possible the rumor of the black warrior ninja women was true, but Miyako knew they were hoping to avoid being seen. No woman in Japan wore all black to get a man to look at her and want her. Dressing this way alongside Shinju made her feel like she was part of a special club. One filled with more sexy soldiers than the two of them could ever grow tired of.

At first, Miyako tried to copy Shinju's style of dress. Miyako admired Shinju's crisp shirts, dresses, and skirts. All black. The red lipstick, the dark curly hair, the loud high heels accentuating every move, were all things Miyako aspired to emulate as well. But she was still borrowing Shinju's clothes, and while Shinju offered Miyako a black garment, she forced her into adding some color.

"Trust me," Shinju told Miyako after she asked for a black dress instead of a blue one. "You can't look exactly like me. Clients want something different in you. Plus, you look good with some color. During the day, you need to stand out. Be sexy in a different way than me. But at night, you can dress more like me. Men can't see what we're wearing as well in the dark. By the time they can see us in the light at night, they're too horny to care."

She loved the sounds her heels made as she walked. They marked her presence. It was her way of announcing to the world she was there. She wouldn't be invisible any longer. Her clicking feet announced to the men she was near and ready for love, while telling the rest of Japan, she was openly enjoying living a life of pleasure.

The way Shinju coached Miyako to do her makeup ensured she stood out. In a crowd, she would be seen. But besides drawing clients, it also made her feel like she was showing off. She wanted everyone to know that she was having a good time.

Those black clothes made her feel powerful. Desired. Sexy. Wanted.

Emotions she'd never felt before.

After a short time, Miyako realized she wanted variety in how she dressed. Shinju was right. She looked good in color. Miyako's skin would appear to glow in the light when she wore the right hue.

Aside from Shinju's color suggestion, Miyako took charge of what she wore, now that she could for the first time. She was excited by the prospect of creating how she looked. She was her own calligraphy, her own painting.

If she felt this good in Shinju's clothes, how would she feel in her own? With the money she made, she bought new things to wear and started choosing other colors, ones Shinju hadn't even suggested.

During the day, she'd wear sunny yellows, sky blues, and cherry blossom pinks. Miyako found dresses with lace and flowers that she took time to label. Dresses with polka dots and cherries. Dresses which were playful and vibrant. It was as if they had a life of their own. At night, she'd wear gray or black. She still almost matched

Shinju in the dark. This comforted her as she experimented with her fashion choices during the daylight.

She'd taken a fancy to hats, ribbons, and shoes. She loved playing with all the different styles. This was a chance to try different ways of expressing herself. Sometimes her clients would praise her for what she was wearing. It was all so intimate to her. These things would hug her naked body for hours, caressing her despite their stillness. They held her most personal parts equally to the rest of her. By picking the clothes that made her feel beautiful and sexy, she proved to herself all of her body was beautiful and well-loved. The clothes she loved, loved her back. They loved her body. She loved her body since it was the source of all of her greatest pleasures. The pleasure of finding the right clothes at the store didn't quite beat sex, but it came close.

***

Shinju taught Miyako different ways to cut her hair. How to layer her hair, and how to give herself bangs if she wanted them. How to curl her hair. Shinju did touch Miyako a little only to show her how to do it right, then left her to do it all on her own once she mastered the techniques. She warned Miyako not to cut her hair too short, however. Men wanted a woman looking feminine.

"They've been around plenty of men during the war," Shinju said as she slid the scissors through Miyako's hair. "They're here to be with ladies. They need to be sure we have vaginas."

That worked to Miyako's benefit anyway. She loved expressing her femininity.

Learning to use curlers was delightful. Miyako's parents would have never let her curl her hair, and now she could do it all how she wanted. Sleeping with the curlers in her hair overnight was something to get used to, but Miyako reminded herself it was nothing compared to how

Geishas slept to keep their hair beautiful. Miyako wouldn't have to sleep with her neck on a painful pedestal and hope she didn't slip off in the night. She could enjoy the comfort of her pillow, letting the curlers work for her as she slept in the daylight, filling her nights as she saw fit. With no wax in her hair to keep it in typical Japanese fashion, she could still bathe! No matter how wild her nights and men, all it took was an overnight rest with the curlers in her hair again, no matter where her head went in the night.

***

Beauty was something Miyako could make work for herself as opposed to her having to work for it. She used beauty as a way to achieve how she wanted to look, instead of how she was supposed to appear. She no longer had clothes or hairstyles which made her feel ugly or didn't show who she wanted to be. She found styles she loved that worked for her and draw the right kind of men to her. Who would take them off and fuck her into happy oblivion?

Makeup contained magic with similar perks. Her painted face revealed a deeper, more profound expression in which her hair and clothes didn't. Lovingly, Miyako matched colors on her face to what she wore, perhaps adding focus to a flower lingering on the cloth near her breast or bring out the blackness around her neck. Shinju taught her very little about makeup, only how to apply lipstick, eye shadow, and blush. There was more to painting up her face as Miyako learned.

Through the colors on her face, Miyako could express her moods and whatever else she wanted to show of herself to potential clients. She could paint her face to show her flirtation, her sexual appetite, her desire to be mysterious. She could show off her current obsession with red or blue, even portray herself like a cherry blossom or a fox if she so desired.

She could hide behind makeup if she wanted to. Hide her past, hide her heritage, hide her embarrassment for what her men had done, even, hide her country's failure. It gave her the comfort to show her face on the days she lost her confidence in what she was doing. The days she wondered if the Americans were only using her.

But, Miyako felt confident when she saw herself in her clothes, shoes, makeup, and hairstyles. A mirror was all she needed to give her the bravery to quench her sexual appetite for handsome men and large cocks.

Miyako delighted in the knowledge that her family would hate what she was wearing. She was looking like an American. Her Japanese roots were behind her. She never liked how she looked in Japanese clothes. No one ever made her feel beautiful when she was forced to look and live in the traditional way. But the American men loved complimenting her on her looks now that she was dressing to their liking. They were the source of her makeover after all.

Miyako liked how she looked for the first time. She looked more like herself than ever before. She loved how her hairstyles framed her face. She liked wearing clothes showing off her prettiest parts. She loved showing off the shape of her breasts and hips, yet leaving enough mystery to entice a man into bed to see the rest. She'd never been able to show off her legs before, but with the American style, they were available for all the men to see. Her heels helped accentuate their sculpted shape as well. When she stole looks at herself in the mirror, she knew why these handsome men wanted to have sex with her. Through fashion, they shaped her into an empress, a goddess, a work of art, the master of sexual pleasure for the American soldier themselves.

***

Miyako feared the Americans at first. Feared they would take out their anger over the war on her. She wasn't sure if being a woman would help. If these men would wish to protect or love her, knowing she too suffered because of the Japanese soldiers. Or would they take revenge for the wrongs of the war through her? Would they take advantage of her naked body and force her to suffer for the sins of her men? Or if she was merely a playmate, a masturbation tool to make them forget the war. Fucking to kill time until they could go home.

She braced herself during each encounter for the worse her imagination could conjure. Would they slit her throat and drink her blood before her dying eyes? Would they cut off her head and screw her corpse? Would they shoot her dead before she could even know what happened? Was it possible to be fucked to death? But these feelings would drift away with most of the men since they treated her so well. Their talk and lovemaking soothed her worries. They wanted her for pleasure as much as she desired them, perhaps even more.

However, if a man scared her, she'd leave them. She assumed men like that hadn't planned on paying or pleasing her anyway. Those weren't real men. Miyako only wanted to fuck real men.

There was a rush that coursed through her when trouble was near. It moved from her stomach to her throat. It would start as a jolt and then linger like frost on a cold day. Her heart would beat faster as a result. The intensity of it would grow when something, or someone, around was especially bad. Her family taught her to believe such feelings were stupid. Her parents would scold her, and her siblings would make fun of her. Deep down she'd always known otherwise, and each time her feelings proved to be right. She knew this warning system, this power to her, would serve her well now. Especially, considering her job.

While many of the men were nice, they weren't all full of desires for pure romance. That horrid sensation inside her alerted her to the men of ill intent. Even if Shinju urged her on, Miyako still wouldn't subject herself to him.

If this kind of man resisted Miyako's departure, she'd turn to dramatics. She would scream and curse. Publicly state why they held no right to her. Making such a scene was usually more than enough for the man to move on. In the few cases, it wasn't, another man would come to her aid. Miyako's rudeness served her well.

***

One time, Shinju brought Miyako to meet two clients who were particularly rough. After the way one of them put his hands near her vagina, Miyako went home without even saying good-bye to either man or Shinju. When Shinju returned in the morning to the apartment they shared, she said nothing to Miyako about skipping out. Miyako only noticed the next evening Shinju's bruises as she patted makeup over them. Shinju was broken inside. When Miyako asked Shinju what happened, she said they fucked like animals. They'd taken turns with her since Miyako left. Miyako didn't press Shinju for anything more. She knew enough about what she left behind. More than worth the loss of income that night.

These kinds of things would continue to happen to Shinju time and again. She would come home with cuts and bruises while seemingly burying some great sorrow. But she would only respond to Miyako's questions with a few words. Sometimes, it seemed Shinju cared more about money than her safety. Maybe she enjoyed the danger, the kind of sex she had with these men. Still, Miyako knew these men didn't care about Shinju. She feared for her.

Maybe Shinju didn't have the same magic gift as Miyako. Her protective sense. Perhaps she ignored it to collect more American dollars. Even the times Miyako tried to warn her about a man, Shinju ignored her.

***

Miyako was in a position to choose her own clients, and she used her feelings to pick the right ones. Miyako kept some of the Americans Shinju had given her, but she found more nice men on her own. Clients who Shinju had no interest in and claimed to be boring. Miyako's dates and bedroom escapades proved otherwise.

Her gut feeling allowed her to predict who would be good in bed and who wouldn't. Since great sex was a priority to her, she learned how to tell which client would prove worthy. Her groin and heart always guided her well in this. The amount of heat a man inspired in her. Her heart and loins would scream yes he's the one. He can take you to the amazing paradise of pleasure.

If she didn't feel turned on, she moved on to someone else. She picked her clients according to this system.

***

Despite the changes Miyako was undergoing, the undressing and discarding of her own culture, she felt more herself than ever before. The potential danger mattered to her less and less as she realized how much fun she was having. She learned ways to protect herself. Even if she hadn't, she would continue anyway. Her freedom mattered more. She was free! Free for the first time. She was free to have sex. Free to curse as loud if not louder than Shinju. It didn't matter if the men laughed or if she got dirty looks from down the street. She could let whatever she wanted slip from her mouth. She could scream about how horny she was or how huge her favorite client's cock was. How she loved her breasts and what had been done to her asshole the night before. How happy she was to be free of the pains Japan gave her and enjoy the pleasures of the Americans.

She didn't have to be friendly to anyone. If a client didn't like her, she'd find another. Usually, her new find was more handsome anyway. She'd even stick her tongue at her scorned ex while she was displayed on the arm of his replacement, and laugh when her dropped man would scowl. She had nothing to fear as she influenced her new man to punch the old one in the face and knock him to the ground if he tried to touch her. Her Americans would always protect her.

Miyako was free from the scrutiny of the Japanese. What did dirty looks and mean words matter? They couldn't touch her. She was above them now. They were still hungry and starving. They hadn't found a way to survive. She had more money than her old Japanese village combined.

The men proved incompetent and the women chose not to do anything to help themselves. Gender was no excuse for the women not getting past the failures of their men. Men who continued to hold them back when they failed them. They were dead, even if many of them were still walking around acting as if they still belonged to the world of the living. They were just jealous. Miyako found a way to not only survive, but thrive in her newfound freedom through Shinju, and through the Americans. They were unworthy of Miyako's pity or thought.

Miyako was free to walk down the street and roam wherever she desired. There was no one to answer to. No one to ask her where she was going or tell her it was too dangerous to be alone. Shinju didn't care as long as she was around to take clients when needed. She could rediscover her new Japan through their eyes. She could finally explore the parts of Japan she always wanted to see. She would finally be able to go to the Cherry Blossom Festival her family never took her to. She could go to any restaurant and try as much American food as she desired. She could go to the beach to put her feet in the sand and gaze into the ocean all day. Though she was disappointed that Shinju would rarely join her, her dates did sometimes.

For the first time in her life, she could do anything she wanted whenever she wanted. A life of her own to cherish and fill with all the things she wanted, including love and sex. Lots of it. Anything which displeased her was quickly discarded to make room for something or someone she loved.

Miyako never thought sleeping with the enemy could feel so good. They weren't really the enemy, just regular men who proved better than the Japanese. Miyako was happy the Americans won the war. They saved her. They kept her alive and gave her a new and better life.

***

Miyako was open to doing just about anything to please the clients she liked. She let them put their penises in her mouth. She was confused by the gesture at first, not understanding why a man would put a penis there. Shinju hadn't mentioned this to her. But the men seemed to love it, and Miyako took to it quickly. She giggled a lot at first, but soon found pleasure in it for herself. She was able to move back and forth as if she was having sex while making out with a huge cock at the same time. It made her so horny. The sex afterward felt more fruitful. Though she quickly learned, she wasn't always in the mood for what the Americans called, a blow job. But she could negotiate. She'd give one in return for something else. Or she could put it off until a man returned the sexual favor. This proved to be a powerful bargaining chip for attaining the pleasures she really desired from the Americans.

She let the soldiers put their penis in both her lower regions. She enjoyed both. She loved when a man went to each place within her in the same night. As if they couldn't get enough of her. Needing to possess her, all of her, every part, even if only for the night.

They'd suck on her neck and bite her. Miyako would do it right back. They'd smack her butt. Pull her hair. Fondle her breast. Stroke and suck her nipples. Mirroring these same actions back on the men didn't seem to go over as well for most of them. But a few of them enjoyed it.

Miyako soon learned people differed in how they gave and experienced pleasure. She learned to be acutely aware of what each man liked and disliked. This ensured each sexual encounter was better than the last, building great and greater pleasures. It also kept clients coming back.

She'd note each man's sexual drive to ensure she continued being the best she could for her client. Especially their more exotic fantasies and preferences. She wanted to ensure the men kept coming to please her, instead of someone else. She wanted to possess their love as long as she could.

Almost every night, and many times it was several times in a night, she would feel a blooming within her. A sense of something was rushing out of her while something beautiful swam inside. A feeling of pleasure beyond anything she had ever known possible before. As if she reached the top of Mount Fiji. It made her feel as if she entered the heavens and returned to Earth again.

One of the men explained to her what it was called. The Orgasm was something she wanted to experience again.

She was delighted that many of the men she encountered wanted her to experience this with them and did whatever they could to ensure it would happen.

Miyako asked Shinju if she ever experienced one herself. Shinju gave her a funny look and told her she didn't think such a thing was possible as Miyako described it.

***

Sex was very involved for some men. She didn't know a person could be tied up in so many different ways. There were all kinds of different knots and ways they could bind her to their whim using rope, ribbon, or whatever else. A man even used shoelaces from his old military boots. Another handcuffs. One even taught her how to tie these kinds of knots herself to use on them.

She loved having her way with this man who had chosen to be helpless to her sexual whims. Each time she used her mouth on his dick until he couldn't take it anymore and begged for her. Then, after forcing him to give her oral pleasure, she would finally satisfy their hunger.

More often though, she found these were the kind of men would tie her to the bed and blindfold her as they had their way with her. At first, this scared her, she felt as if she was losing some of her own free will again like when she was still a real Japanese girl. But she agreed to such activities because she wanted a thrill. The thrill of going too far only to find the ultimate of pleasures. Choosing to partake in such activities with clients, she trusted made all the difference. She did such things with clients who had earned her trust and deserved to have her body entirely.

These men were powerful enough to hurt her, even kill her. Submitting to them made her even more aware of this. What once scared her now turned her on immensely. She felt that powerful energy within them when they made love, and she sucked it in, hoping it would linger with her and somehow make her strong, too. This lit her up to the point that she felt the thoughts themselves could cause orgasms before she was even touched.

She went deeper and deeper into what she was willing to do, her rules of sex becoming more and more fluid to the point there were barely any rules at all. She knew she'd be safe as she explored her fears and pleasures with them.

Some of the men liked keeping it light when it came to sexual explorations. Upon becoming naked, Miyako and her clients would make love to each other right then and there. Or, some would still take their time with her. Some would massage her back and other areas before having sex. They loved giving pain relief for discomfort she never even knew she had. Pains that started long before the war.

Some would draw words on her stomach, thighs, and breast with their tongue. Others would use their tongues on the part of her that bloomed when she was excited. This was her second favorite sexual experience. She loved feeling men making out with her vagina. She orgasmed so fast this way that she exploded all over the faces of those who loved her. One man told her he was happy to know there was no way she could have ever faked that. Apparently, his previous lovers never gave him enough of a chance to orgasm with him. Miyako was honored by this and encouraged him that she could do the same things with future lovers. Still, she'd possessed him as long as she could.

Her favorite deed was penis to vagina lovemaking though. The only way Miyako thought both parties could experience the full package each of their bodies provided. When skin pressed against skin. She orgasmed so easily, and then usually multiple times. It was one of the few times she'd felt truly safe, a sense of belonging.

She hadn't been cared for as well by her own family. Embraced in the arms of strangers, caressed by the enemy. In the end, they weren't the enemy after all. They were heroes. They'd won the war. Stopped the Japanese men who had held her back. The family who didn't love her. They were the ones who'd given Miyako and Shinju their new lives. The ones giving her all the money, gifts, and pleasures. They didn't trap her as she'd been with her family. She had her own life now, and she could serve herself. Serving them was a choice. She was rewarded greatly for all of this. She hadn't received anything for her previous loyalty to her family. She was happy to have abandoned them. She'd been rewarded with great treasure.

***

Miyako felt adored by these men. Serving them was part of her pleasure as well. She chose her men carefully, only the ones worthy of her.

"Don't pick anyone who looks sick, poor, or stupid," Shinju said. "If they try to speak Japanese to pick you up, drop them. And don't pick anyone who is already drunk, they won't remember to pay you."

Why didn't Shinju take her own advice?

Miyako wanted each night to be magical, full of orgasms. While some nights didn't live up to this expectation, many of them did. Orgasms came easy to her when she let go and succumbed to the pleasure of the moment. Without judgment on what thoughts or sensations brought her to ecstasy, she found anything, and everything held some kind of beauty.

She couldn't believe this much fun in life was possible. Perhaps these were things only Americans did. Perhaps the Japanese were the only ones who didn't. She didn't know, but she now enjoyed these forbidden treasures.

***

Miyako loved her power of choice. She chose what to wear, where to go, and who to date. She still looked to Shinju for guidance and approval. But after a series of many questions Shinju would roll her eyes and tell Miyako,

"Do whatever the fuck you feel like! I'm not your mother! Just go fuck and make money. Stop making this complicated! Stop annoying me!"

Miyako felt freed by Shinju's words. If she didn't care why should she? She could do whatever she wanted. She hugged Shinju and kissed her on the cheek.

"I love you! Thank you!"

"Get off of me you freak! I told you I never wanted us to touch like that again!"

Had touching Miyako's naked body offended her so deeply? Miyako couldn't understand it. Perhaps women weren't meant to make love. Still, Miyako highly doubted that, but she preferred men anyway.

After that, Miyako only asked her fashion questions.

***

Much of Miyako's power came from money. It seemed to be never-ending no matter how much she spent. Suddenly, she found herself buying all of these pretty things for herself as she had never been able to before. Not one beautiful thing was out of the question for her to have. But Shinju reminded her to save money for food and other necessities.

"I'm not your mother. If you can't eat, you'll starve. You have to take care of your own food. You'll have to take care of your own living situation soon too. You'll need to be able to pay rent each month for your own apartment. Nightly clients are no guarantee. Remember this won't last. At some point, you'll need to have money to live on."

Miyako found Shinju's words to be wise, considering the poverty she survived through. She started to save a portion of her money under her bed. Yet she didn't think the flood of lovers would ever end.

Shinju would still watch Miyako's body intently when she dressed and undressed in her apartment. But she never let Miyako see her naked body. She'd always change somewhere else. Or make Miyako turn away. Miyako wondered why Shinju didn't want to see her naked.

Sometimes she caught Shinju looking at her with longing. Why wouldn't Shinju look her in the eyes as often as she used to, but would still stare at the rest of her? Shinju didn't look at men the same way as Miyako. She smiled well, but her eyes held another emotion entirely. Miyako wasn't sure what though.

But she dared not ask her even though she longed for answers. Maybe one day when she was braver she would finally ask Shinju.

***

As Shinju promised, Miyako was able to afford her own place within a few months. Shinju kicked her out when the time was right. The first time Miyako went on a shopping spree, she bought so many dresses she filled the closet in Shinju's apartment. Miyako returned the next morning to find all of her clothes thrown out the window. It was time.

She found a place rather quickly, considering Shinju's temper. It was much closer to Washington Heights, the American haven, than Shinju's place was. Miyako liked being closer to the culture she was growing to love, whereas Shinju seemed to prefer avoiding Americans when she wasn't working. Miyako could watch all the fashions of the American women there. Buy American things to make her feel like a real American woman. The outside world by her apartment enchanted Miyako's heart, but it was the inside that made it her home.

Her own space between white walls and a wooden floor. A bathroom with a real working toilet and shower. Plumbing a modern convenience brought by the Americans. She would never go back to having a bathroom any other way. She could choose whether to keep her shoes on the inside or not. A kitchen stood in wait, but Miyako knew she would barely use it at all. Cooking would remind her too much of her old life. Restaurants and over the counter snacks were her forms of dining now.

Her bedroom was her favorite place. Her closet was already filled with clothes after a few weeks of moving in. She had stuffed animals, mostly bears, on a dresser that faced her from behind her bed. In the center was a wooden box decorated with cherry blossoms, a gift from Roger, filled with jewelry the soldiers had given her. A mirror loomed over the bed. The mirror allowed her to watch as she made love to a man, or masturbated. Watch herself doing all the things that she felt freed her.

Within the dresser, Miyako kept the sexiest underwear, bras, she bought or was gifted. There were two nightstands on either side of the bed with American style lamps. Her bed was large enough to accommodate the tallest and strongest of men. The sheets were the gray color of the sea after a storm, concealing the wreckage from her lovemaking. Helpful when Miyako forgot to wash them or saw too many clients in a row to do so.

Things could get messy when the men were over, and sometimes Miyako reveled in the disorder.

***

She bought cigarettes but never took the same liking to smoking that Shinju had. Miyako only smoked if a soldier offered her a cigarette or when she needed something to do while waiting for clients. She observed Shinju emptying several packs of Rose and Gion a day. She'd only smoke those American brands, even though she said she hated the taste.

As for alcohol, Miyako was only interested in the girly and floral wines. The sweet drinks. She was impressed with how Shinju was able to take down shot after shot, and she aimed to drink like her. Especially since a high tolerance to alcohol seemed to impress the men.

Though when Miyako tried whiskey, she got the same laughter from the men as she did when she tried to drink soda the first time. It all went to her nose, making her gasp and giggle.

Miyako didn't understand the American obsession with coffee. Shinju taught Miyako to drink it to keep in line with the Americans but also to stay awake after long nights of sex followed by early breakfasts with clients. So many men in the military were always up early, no matter how long they'd been up together the night before. Miyako decided coffee would be an occasional fix, but nothing she could stand too much of. It was too bitter.

***

Miyako held a special love for black men. They were the most gentle and considerate. She loved how their skin tone was rich and dark. Roger seemed to want to stick around.

White men were more adventurous with her in bed though. They also gave her the most expensive gifts. She could schedule with either kind of man based on her sexual moods for that day or week. Both types of men loved their romance and making love. Individuality went beyond skin tone, of course, loving each man was a unique experience.

All of these things she learned in order to be the greatest lover the Americans ever had.

***

Before Miyako knew it, years went by. Never once considering the deeper desires with herself in which she couldn't fulfill, no matter who she had sex with.

1949

Miyako's collection of lovers was a vast ocean, a constant wave of men that both overwhelmed and moved her. As a result, she wrote down all her appointments to ensure she wouldn't double book and get lost in this sea. Miyako was more worried about the insult of standing up an American hero than the loss of income if she accidentally missed a date. Money was something that always flowed freely to her now, but love was something she could never have enough.

Tuesdays were her days with Roger. They usually went to the burger joint, a movie, and then back to her place. Occasionally, they'd travel to the parts of Japan still rooted in its history. He was the only man she'd let see her past. Mondays and Wednesdays were set aside for her other repeat clients and their routines. The rest of the week varied. Yet, her nights held the greatest potential.

Some nights she'd see her repeats. Safe in the cover of night they were free from the confines of their daylight routine. Wild and passionate, their bodies would speak the language of pleasure through fulfilling a fantasy. Other nights she'd meet new men. Those were the most exciting, yet unpredictable nights. She'd meet these men free of inhibition, gambling with hope and danger. Caught only by imagination and limitations of the body, she could dive in more deeply with strangers. Reaching depths her other clients feared. It was her chance to fall in love again.

As Miyako's country was remodeled by the Americans, the land itself stayed the same but businesses and people transformed. Some bustling and magical. However, some stayed resentful even after the war. Miyako thought poorly of those individuals. Her post-war life had given her something her own people and country hadn't ever provided her. Actual fun.

Miyako noted in her book which dresses, shoes, and pieces of jewelry each GI bought her. She wore them for the appropriate client. She noted her lover's favorite colors, hairstyles, perfume preferences, and whether they enjoyed a woman's painted face or naked skin. She carefully planned her attire for her repeat clients in order to ensure their pleasure. Not only was this vital for business, but it was needed to ensure her own pleasure. Miyako knew she would be rewarded for her efforts. Financially and sexually. She remembered their favorite foods and activities as well as personal details and stories they told her. On dates, she incorporated inside jokes and activities reserved for one particular client. She needed each client to believe he was the center of her world, if only while sharing a table or bed.

Miyako learned through her line of work of sexual variety that not all men enjoyed the same things in bed. She memorized preferred positions, turn ons, and turn offs of her soldiers. She directed each sexual encounter for the highest pleasure of her clients and herself.

In return, she always received an abundance of gifts from her lovers. Beautifully crafted chocolates with mysterious flavors, pretty things to wear, instruments in which she was responsible to unlock their music, sex toys which Miyako was eager to use again and again, drawings of herself which flattered her figure and ego, rosy gums, photographs of her lovers, exotic smelling perfumes, chewy jerkies, stuffed animals, and even a slinky. She loved her treasures and guarded them as if they were family.

Miyako was a collector of American GI's love. What else could she ever want out of life? She was willing to become immortal if it meant being loved by and loving these men forever. A beautiful eternity of romance.

***

The time right before and during the start of her period was a real bummer for Miyako. All of her raging emotions fighting to escape like big fists beating her insides to make sure they were noticed. Soreness tearing her down. All of the blood which oozed from her dark insides. She felt it everywhere, with no comfort or relief.

Back in her old life, none of this was talked about. Miyako was never allowed to express herself during these times even though all she wanted to do was scream and cry. Her mother told her to act as if it didn't exist. Miyako resented her for it.

Early on in her training, Shinju had brought Miyako back to her place after a date was running late. Shinju complained her period just started, and she knew her underwear was already soaked in blood. All she wanted to do was be home eating chocolate in bed. Miyako was shocked Shinju was being so open about something she'd kept in the dark for so long. Shinju screamed at her to get off as she always did when they touched when Mikayo hugged her.

From then on, Miyako and Shinju talked openly about their trials with the bloodies. It was nice to not hide it anymore. It was nothing to be ashamed of, as it was something all women experienced. Of course, they could speak about it. Shinju and Miyako would laugh and cry together. Bitch over how bad it was. Miyako was free from shame at last.

Miyako could scream down the street or cry at the movie theater. She could binge on chocolate or down several hamburgers. If she wanted a break from eating, that was fine too. If she wanted to spend the day at home and do nothing, there was no problem. She could express herself however she wanted to. She was free. Miyako knew that's how it should have been among women all along.

Plus, Shinju knew a few tricks to make the whole process easier. Eating chocolate seemed to help. Shinju also taught Miyako too much sweetness was bad, but just enough would relieve the tiredness as long as she drank tea or coffee. Shinju also advised the magic of just sleeping it all away. Of course, sex provided relief as well.

The soldiers made it all better too. They seemed all the more tender during her bloody time. They'd give her chocolates and massages, told her tricks that worked with their wives and girlfriends. Most would still have sex with her. This lessened the pain while reminding her she was still sexy even if her vagina turned into a bloody volcano. Any man who was grossed out by this, she could reschedule when her warm lava finished its course. Sex proved once again a perfect celebration. Feeling a man before his own eruption proved her own body's processes were natural as well. Women just erupted in two ways; a slow painful red and a fleeting beautiful white.

***

Over the years, Miyako honed in on her fashion style through observing the American women who came through Washington Heights. At first, she thought she wanted to be them, but she realized she just wanted to look like them. The American men were coming to her after all; the American women who found themselves in her turf weren't enough. Miyako held their sexual drives hostage. She wasn't losing control any time soon. Knowing the styles of beauty her soldiers were accustomed to would only help maintain her romantic hold.

Miyako kept her mascara thick and dramatic as Shinju taught her when she first started. But she learned to keep her eyeshadow more subtle than Shinju's. She wanted her lips to stand out instead. Her lips, which would smile, laugh, and move in ways to allude to a man how they would please him.

Miyako matched her lipsticks to whatever dress she wore. With a growing assortment of clothes and colors to choose from, her lipsticks also needed to keep up. Red to orange, pink to purple, and even blue. Miyako especially loved wearing blue lipstick. Not the blue of the daytime sky, but a color that was richer, deeper. The night blue of the American flag, a sapphire from a GI, or found on a U.S. soldier's uniform. This was the hue Miyako loved. Blue made her feel otherworldly, truly a creature of the night. Preparing her to live up to sexual expectations.

Miyako repainted her nails several times a week in order to match all of her changing fashion moods and client preferences. She especially loved pairing her fingers and lips with the same blue hue. Blue was her exception when it came to pairing it with clothes. For her, blue belonged with everything. A color which found itself caressing anything worthy of pleasure before finding its way inside.

Miyako's signature was a blue kiss. She always carried blue lipstick in her bag even if she wasn't wearing any. Secretly, she'd plant a blue kiss in an intimate spot only her lover would find. His coffee cup while he cooked eggs in her kitchen, his underwear while he slept, his extra condom still neatly wrapped after a night of lovemaking using another. Miyako left a lingering presence of the romance they shared long after her lips left anything of his.

Blue also represented what Americans brought to her country. The Japanese and American flags were red and white. But America brought a third color, blue, to represent the night sky which held the stars in place. Blue represented the night Miyako loved. Which held possibility and freedom.

Blue was deep, mysterious, exotic. Adorning herself in this color dressed her in these qualities. The color gave her a sense of safety as did the Americans did, shielding against the pains of her past. She gave her absolute trust to the Americans as well as her willingness to let them take everything from her.

***

Miyako wore rounded sunglasses compared to the squarish ones of Shinju. If she lost some confidence, from double guessing her color coordination or jitters about a new man, she would put on her frames and instantly feel better even if it was already dark outside. Her mood always seemed to lighten.

Shinju's nails and lips were always red, and her eye makeup always black. This hadn't changed over the years. Miyako made suggestions to Shinju to try new looks with her. But Shinju always denied her.

Shinju maintained few long-term clients. None of them were gentlemen. Miyako knew she was a better lover than Shinju. Miyako knew her men inside and out, she studied them. Did whatever she could to discover every small detail they hid from the rest of the world. Things they were embarrassed about masturbating to. How they were secretly thrilled when their girlfriend cheated on them with another woman, how the sight of pink flowers made them horny, their curiosities about other men. Because of this, Miyako could fulfill their desire in ways no one else could.

Yet Miyako felt there was so much more sexual territory to explore in order to continue rising as the greatest of lovers.

Miyako wanted Shinju to touch her as she had years ago. Miyako wanted the full experience of being with a woman. Rather than being sexually attracted to Shinju, Miyako wanted the experience out of the way to appease curiosity. Happily, she'd return to only fucking men, her questions about sex between females answered.

Shinju hadn't seen Miyako naked in years. Miyako hadn't caught Shinju looking at her like she used to. She wondered if, despite that, Shinju was curious about what it would be like to have full sex with a woman as well. If it was true Shinju never orgasmed before, Miyako could teach her how. That way, Shinju could enjoy her clients even better. Seek pleasure through them as Miyako did. Perhaps this would result in Shinju picking better men for the sake of her own safety and enjoyment.

Miyako longed to ask Shinju about this. Ask Shinju if she would just once let them explore each other. Miyako's boldness toward men grew each day. Yet, her courage to ask Shinju even a simple question, never mind one so big, continued to diminish.

Shinju became increasingly snappy over the years, and less playful. Shinju would go out of her way to not even look at Miyako in any way. She couldn't remember the last time they'd made eye contact. She acted as if Miyako was an annoyance rather than a friend or coworker in the business of the night.

***

Miyako didn't have many females to pass time with. None for fashion shopping or trying new styles in makeup using the newest shades. None to giggle and talk about hot men with. Answer the carnal questions she dared not ask Shinju. Shinju wouldn't do any of those things with her. Miyako only saw her now if Shinju needed to schedule a double date with her. Using Miyako only to avoid losing money.

Miyako tried to make friends with other women, but it was all in vain. They called her slut and whore, traitor to Japan. Or they'd ignore her entirely. Everything she did seemed to fuel women's hatred of her.

A few times, the soldiers would ask Japanese girls for directions. Miyako intervened since they didn't know English like she did. While the men appreciated it, the women would sneer at her, and call her names when the American got far away enough. If she managed to snag a client out of it, the women would scowl as she walked away with her new lover in tow.

Miyako felt their hatred. Their hope that she would disappear into the night from which she came, never to return. But Miyako would never abandon her lovers like that, even if it made women angry. Miyako believed it was only because they were jealous of her and didn't care about what made American men happy.

But with all the women envying her and competing for business, or perhaps just male attention, Miyako knew she was among the best of lovers for the Americans. Perhaps she was the best already, she hadn't met anyone who could draw and keep a man like she could. And good men at that.

Miyako didn't understand other women, though. She didn't feel like she belonged to her own gender, she was too much of an outsider. Women didn't want her. Men did. Men allowed her in. The American ones at least. But she hadn't been able to connect with any American women. They shut her out just like the Japanese women. Would it be so much trouble to share a night with her? Men were friends with each other, why couldn't she make friends with women?

Many of the same women who gave her death stares often were dressing like Miyako the next time she saw them. They were missing the basics that created a great outfit, like bright lipstick and nail polish. While still giving her death stares, their desperation and disdain rose to the surface. Yet, Miyako was still the one who won the real American heroes. Soon her copies would disappear entirely. Miyako would have felt bad if they hadn't been so mean to her in the first place. Nasty women couldn't love anywhere near as well as she.

Then there were the feminists. They were more aggressive in their approach. Together in a chorus of screams and signs, they'd preach how Miyako needed to change her ways. They'd throw trash at her while screaming what a disgrace to all women she was. Their anger and hunger seemed to fuel themselves while it'd broken other women. Shinju would have her fun yelling right back at them. Telling them how dried up they were on the inside and to die with the rest of Japan. Miyako didn't understand how such women could possibly be standing up for her gender. Their claims held no water in her eyes. Yet, they survived Japan while other women perished.

The only female in Mikayko's life that didn't hate her was Shinju. Her only real friend. Shinju who hid so much of herself even with Miyako.

Perhaps being a lover of men made women unable to love you. Perhaps that's why Shinju wouldn't be with her again. Miyako wasn't sure.

***

"Those colors are too light for you," Shinju told Miyako as they stood outside the movie theater.

"But I love peaches!" said Miyako. "Drew seems to like the colors too. He said his favorite dessert was cream and peaches. Or peach pie. My dress and makeup will make him want to gobble me up the same way."

Shinju rolled her eyes, "Gross. Did a man really say that to you? Must you always copycat all of these mens' likes?"

"I get better presents when I do!" said Miyako. "And more money."

"But you need to appeal to the most men," said Shinju.

"Even when I'm on a date with my client?"

"At some point, your beloveds are going to go back to America and you'll need new ones. Sometimes a new client might present himself while you're with someone else. Jealousy of another man having you one night could put his money in your pocket the next."

Miyako smiled. "I always manage to get new lovers. I have my ways."

Miyako proceeded to pull out her blue lipstick and swipe it across her lips. She blew a kiss at Shinju.

Shinju snorted.

Miyako didn't respond to Shinju. She noticed Shinju lost some weight and there was a small tear in the back of her dress and rips in her stocking. This was unheard of for Shinju. Since the time they'd met, Shinju had been an impeccable dresser. A crisp black beauty.

"You have holes." Miyako nodded her head and shifted her eyes at each one.

Shinju sneered. "I'm meeting up with Tom. He takes off my clothes so fast he never notices what I'm wearing anyway. I don't want to let him ruin anymore of my good clothes with those oversized hands of his."

Miyako sighed and lit a cigarette. She'd finished with Roger in the morning, so she was meeting up with Drew, the only musician she was currently seeing. There weren't too many artists in Miyako's life, so she appreciated his talents. She'd only met up with him a few times, but it was always a magical time. Every night they shared, he would play his violin for her. Arousal bewitched her as she watched his hands move over the body of the instrument, coaxing it to make sounds of its own. Afterward, Miyako was his instrument. Together they created beautiful music with their bodies. His hands forced her to make sounds she'd never made before, sounds she didn't know she was capable of before. Music only for him.

Tom picked up Shinju and she didn't even say good-bye to Miyako. Clenching her jaw in response, Miyako stewed in her annoyance. Drew appeared a few minutes later and only then did her smile return. After a long make out session, which didn't feel quite like usual even though she was still riding the highs of it, the pair entered the movie theater.

The screen flashed some kissing scene that Miyako already seen with three other clients, so she wasn't paying attention to the movie. Drew took all of her focus. Normally, he'd already be working his hand under her dress, pulling down her underwear to stroke her insides. Tonight he was rigid and his eyes miles away. He barely touched her, only tracing his fingers up and down her arm. Miyako felt a great sadness for him. She was determined to heal him of the storm brewing within his slate eyes.

They stopped to eat after at the usual burger joint. Miyako watched Drew the whole time, recycling the usual comments which got him talking: what life would be like when he was finally a famous musician, how many records he would mail back to Japan for her, how excited Miyako was to be his instrument for the night. But all this pulled out of him was a word or two. Miyako sat across from him in silence and defeat. Two full plates proving her failure.

As they walked toward the hotel, Miyako debated blowing him to send him to sleep. She'd be free to find another lover for the night. Someone easier. But Miyako resolved to find a way to love the pain out of him. Drew deserved that.

When they reached their room and sat on the bed together, Drew pulled a large case from underneath them. The worn one, which had been thrown around by a drunk friend of his. Luckily, it was empty at the time. Miyako knew this case and what it hid well. He opened it and revealed the violin he often played for her. Miyako couldn't imagine he was in the mood to play now.

Miyako took off her clothes and laid next to the violin. She remained there for a while until Drew spoke.

"I never showed you a picture of my girl, have I?" Drew said.

Miyako shook her head. "I'd like to see her." It was the first genuine smile she'd been able to give him all night. A smile that wasn't hopelessly masking her distress at his pain which she couldn't remedy. Drew pulled out his wallet. As he handed Miyako the money he owed her, he passed over a photo of a beautiful blonde curly-haired women wearing a bathing suit at the beach. She was laying herself across a towel on the sand. She appeared to be laughing. Round sunglasses, reminding Miyako of her own, rested on top of her head.

"She's beautiful!" Miyako exclaimed. "Just like a movie star!"

Drew tucked the picture back into his wallet and Miyako slipped away her money. Somehow, he seemed more morose now.

"She's dead," he said quietly. "I just found out today. It's my fault."

"How could something like that be your fault?"

"She was tired of being alone, tired of waiting for me to come home. I just got the letter today. She died three weeks ago."

"But you're an American hero! You're here to make everything better for everyone. Heroes don't hurt people. She didn't have to wait much longer for you, did she?"

"Miyako, she's dead and you're not helping."

Miyako grew silent, being unsure of what else to say.

"I need you to take this violin." he said. "This is the last thing in the world I care about and you're the closest thing to a friend I've got here. The other soldiers will wreck it when they get drunk enough. I don't have family left that I can trust. Very few know I still make music."

"Friend? I'm your lover!" Miyako chirped.

He frowned. "Perhaps this was a mistake."

"No!" Miyako cried. She hugged the violin and laid it next to herself. Caressing it in the way she couldn't for Drew. She answered more seriously this time, "I will take it and treat it with love!" Miyako opened the case and patted the instrument inside with her blue kiss.

He smiled.

"You do look sexy naked next to that violin.

He closed the violin back in the case.

"Wait, what are you going to play now?" Miyako asked.

"I'm going home. I don't need it anymore."

Another one of Miyako's favorite lovers returning to America, she presumed. She was sad he would be leaving her embrace and not returning to another, but at least he was hers one last time in the darkness.

They made love that night. Drew didn't make music with her body this time. Just sounds of two people in physical intimacy was heard between them. He focused on pleasing her, using his tongue on her blooming parts for what felt like hours. Miyako came twice for him. Drew didn't put his dick in her. Yet even that night, she knew he felt something deeper to it all. Drew was trying to communicate with her, not with his words but through his interaction with her naked body. A musician speaking through silence. An eternity passed between them, each detail etched into Miyako's memory as she awoke the next morning. Drew's body absent from the bed. A single rose and a note underneath the only other proof of the love they shared.

You are the most beautiful part of this strange land. Thank you. Good-bye

Miyako grabbed the case and took it back to her apartment. The feelings inside her so real, she thought she was dreaming.

***

The next three weeks Miyako enjoyed the whirlwind romance of a new lover, Tommy. Big and strong, he reminded her of a bear. Powerful in his movements yet gentle in his approach, Miyako was captive but safe in her infatuation. A laugh warmed her and a penis that completely filled her, Miyako was riding the joys of falling in love again.

By the fourth week, Tommy's joy melted into sadness. Miyako feared their time was ending too soon. But this wasn't the reason for the powerful emotions he struggled to keep at bay. Sitting down for coffee, Miyako found out he was Drew's roommate. Discovering clients knew each other wasn't uncommon, but Miyako knew to play it cool. Each man needed to believe she belonged only to him. Drew was old news, and she wanted to keep Tommy. Though listening to another man confiding about her client unknowingly was something new.

Tommy found Drew hanging from the ceiling of the apartment they shared. The military was taking care of the body so the matter was out of his hands. There was no address to send condolences or flowers. He didn't even know where Drew's body was going, though there were rumors of Arlington for an award he'd won. Miyako pretended to understand. Drew hadn't mentioned any award to her. She'd ask another client what Arlington meant later, for now she let Tommy keep talking.

Her last night with Drew was finally making sense.

Tommy confessed to not knowing of Drew's plan and guilt of not reaching him sooner. As he spoke, it became clear to Miyako at the time of Drew's death, Tommy was with her.

Miyako didn't want to upset her client. She hid most of her emotions away. Revealed just enough to show shock and sympathy at the discovery. Showed what people could feel for a stranger, but not enough to prove she was his lover.

Did love kill? Drew claimed his lover's love for him ended her life. He ended his life in turn. Miyako missed the warning signs that stood out in her memory painfully clear now. She failed to save him. Was she the reason Tommy failed to save him to? Begging him for one more ride to orgasm, making Tommy climax so hard he'd slept in her apartment instead of going home? Which act of hers allowed Drew to die?

"When was this?" Miyako asked.

"Monday morning."

Miyako's guilt was sealed. She'd held Tommy captive to her large sexual appetite Sunday night and by Monday morning, she still hadn't had her fill of him. It didn't take too much persuasion on her part to get him erect again. By the time he left, Miyako was slipping into the happy sleep of post-orgasmic bliss.

In his last moments, did Drew think of Miyako or his American lover? She'd never know.

Either way, she'd been screwing another man as he died. Suffered as she orgasmed with the one who could have made it home just in time to stop him, if Miyako hadn't been so greedy in her sexual drive.

Miyako could easily get swallowed into her guilt if she let herself get swept away in it.

Instead, she focused on the man in front of her.

She needed to give herself to him fully. This was still her job.

She grabbed Tommy's hand and pulled him along until they were safety hidden away in her apartment.

Even as she presented her naked body to Tommy, the pain inside of not saving Drew made her feel unworthy of being loved again. But once Tommy was inside of her, her thoughts were taken away from the dreadful place of death and regret. He broke into her pain, reaching into her deepest parts beyond the physical means of sex. Despite not knowing her sorrow, he somehow touched upon her truth through reaching her most tender parts. Joining her through their mutual regret over the same man, even if one of them didn't know it.

Tommy placed something beautiful instead, warm and loving. Giving Miyako hope her love still meant something to these men. Hope and love could still heal even in a world where sometimes someone didn't get saved. Because love would always be there to heal and comfort where it could be felt. He rescued her from her sadness, a true American hero.

The next morning, she kissed him for a long time. Every part of his body was covered by her lips. She couldn't speak her gratitude but hoped he could still feel it deep inside. Perhaps she'd taken some of Tommy's pain as well. He seemed lighter when he left. He didn't laugh but at least he was smiling.

Miyako spent the next few hours in bed before reaching under her bed for a pair of shoes. Her hands swept across Drew's violin. Miyako forgotten she put it there. Pain flooded back as blood rushed into her heart. She took a long breath. It was too late for Drew. She'd never hear his music again, not while lying next to him in bed or from a record delivered by mail. His dreams were over. He killed them himself.

There were still so many men she needed to love. Love could still save someone else. Miyako resolved herself to save through the power of love. Not just for Drew's sake, but for the sake of the other men as well as her own.

***

In Miyako's line of work, there were dangers to avoid.

There were the police raids, which would sweep the night women off the street and into a black hole of unknown horrors. Rumors of experiments at hospitals and executions ran rampant. Luckily, Shinju slept with one of the cops and knew when to avoid certain streets. The police routine became boringly predictable after that. Yet, she once heard screams of a raid right outside her apartment, and the desperate cries of those women unable to escape haunted her dreams.

There were the Feminists. Miyako assumed they were jealous of all the sex, fun, presents, and money she received. Perhaps they were too afraid of American men or weren't pretty enough to get laid, thus wanting to ruin her fun. They were growing in numbers and unlike the police, Miyako and Shinju couldn't track their movements. Their mission to stop the lifestyle Miyako loved was becoming a larger threat since they gained political backing from Japan. Her country was still weak, though. This would serve to her benefit in this matter for a while longer. But she knew those women would eventually become her biggest problem.

Still, it was nothing compared to what her soldiers faced in battle. This gave Miyako courage. If they survived war, she'd be able to overcome anything that came her way.

Miyako heard the horrors of war through her lovers. Terror echoed through their memories. These were not things the Americans were quick to talk about. But sometimes after a night of heavy drinking, the stories would slip past their inhibitions. Stories of pain and death. Stories of all consuming fear. Stories of heroism and triumph: not their own but others. Miyako was quick to put the rest of the pieces together. See where they omitted their own triumphs. Bravest of men were also the most humble. That was one good thing her past life taught her.

Miyako listened as her drunken men talked about the tortures they'd endured under the Japanese. Miyako listened intently. She wouldn't speak in fear as the men would snap out of their alcoholic trance and not tell her anymore. She wanted to know so she could love her clients better. Heal them from their pain. She'd experienced first hand how love could do that. How she was remade and redeemed in the arms of a strong and wonderful man.

She didn't want to fail them like she failed Drew. So, she listened, hoping to learn what she could to take the pain away.

But she was getting pulled into the darkness with them. Sometimes she would wake up at night feeling as if she was suffocating and not remember if she'd been dreaming. Afterward she would shake and cry. If she was with a man that night, they'd often hold her until she stopped crying. If she was alone, she'd hold whatever stuffed animal was close at hand, sometimes several. She'd let the surreality of the feelings wash over her. Even after her men asked why she wept, she couldn't answer. She felt she had no right to cry about other's burdens of the war, but she could cry for those who'd suffered.

The Japanese tried all cost to kill the Americans Any kindness American soldiers showed them was met with death. Many American soldiers died attempting to aid wounded Japanese soldiers to give them a chance to live. Instead, the Japanese killed the Americans. Even in defeat, they wanted as many Americans dead as possible. As a result, the Americans ensured all Japanese were dead at the end of battle, which they hadn't needed to do with enemies from other lands. There could be no survivors this time.

The pointlessness of it infuriated Miyako. The Japanese dragged on the war, while her family starved, while she starved. All the men in her family died because of this. The woman were most certainly dead now too. So many lost families, friends, and lovers. Their own lives. And for what? Because the Japanese couldn't let go of their pride. They wanted to kill everyone so there would be no existing world where their illusions of superiority lay broken. But the Americans won and forced them into seeing the truth instead. Miyako thought it was a fitting punishment.

Miyako wished she wasn't Japanese, but something else instead. She didn't want to associate herself with men who caused her lover's suffering. Her own suffering. The Japanese only made everything worse for everyone.

She couldn't run from her heritage, only hide it, and join a new side. She could make up for the sins of her heritage. Sins she never committed. But she couldn't become an American either. No matter what, she would never fully be an American woman. She was stuck between worlds. But at least she could make her own road. Her own redemption.

Miyako wanted to be the American's reward for surviving. She loved how they didn't identify her as one of the horrible Japanese. She loved that unlike the Japanese, the Americans let her be her own person. They let her be forgiven, something that wasn't part of her old life. They acknowledged she'd chosen to leave a different history of herself. They didn't make her feel as if she owed them anything, and it made her all the more whole. All the more willing to give herself to them completely, be whatever they needed her to be.

For Miyako, there was another reason as well.

War made the best lovers.

War tested a man. It determined if they were a rising hero or bound to fall. It sorted the good from the bad, strong from the weak. Choices made from instinct and courage in the face of fear spoke volumes of who was truly worthy of her love. Love she gave to be forgiven of sins she never committed. She didn't do it for Japan, or the people of her country, but for herself and for these American soldiers.

Miyako previously tried to heal the men damaged by war. But she grew tired of this quickly as Shinju told her she would. They were weak. They would never have saved her if the choice was given. They couldn't fully forgive her. They carried the pain of war, becoming so possessive of it they couldn't trade it for love. They weren't worthy of her time, her love. Miyako pitied them.

She focused instead on the men who were the survivors of war. They were better at taking her in, appreciating all the love and devotion she could provide. They treated her like a forbidden treat which been finally attained. She knew their molding by war was a big part of her love for them.

These men were able to share this time with her, time war created. The beauty, which came after war's ugliness and destruction. In its wake, it created something new, an opportunity for love. Those racing temporary moments of rapture and pleasure. Embracing those fleeting moments. Those men were much better at that. They understood the transience of sex and life, they appreciated her more.

They were beautiful, but dangerous. They needed to be to survive. This added to their appeal.

Perhaps she too was in love with war. War transformed her into a better lover as well. War gave her the opportunity to love in the first place. She wanted to make her mark on the war as it had on her.

Her relationships with these men was more real than anything else she ever had in her village or family. There was depth in sex and depth in their conversation. All other conversations she previously had proved to be shallow. Her old life never allowed her to know anyone, and it hadn't allowed for anyone to understand her. Japanese cared more for being polite and following the hierarchy. In fulfilling roles, there wasn't room to discover who anyone was.

Miyako hadn't been allowed to understand herself. Hadn't been allowed to figure herself out. Her family relations were shallow as with her neighbors. People who would be doomed to isolation from each other and themselves.

War gave her the chance for something new. To really know someone. To connect in their depths through her own. Share her life with them. In sharing herself, she was able to find pieces of herself. What she agreed with and what she disagreed with. Where they shared ground, sorrow, joy. The best part was learning it was okay. The right men loved her for who she was as long as she was being true to herself. She loved them for all their similarities and differences to each other as well as herself.

There were moments she knew they could see into each other's souls. They were sharing their stories and becoming part of each other's stories at the same time.

Miyako couldn't understand why life hadn't been this way all along.

***

Yet, after of all these years of living a life of pure romance, Miyako was unfulfilled. Hollowness growing inside revealed another hunger entirely. At first, she ignored it. She told herself she just needed to find the magic to her life again. Find some new lovers. Be grateful for everything the men given her. Yet soon it became apparent the hunger was coming from somewhere inside which refused to be silenced. It started as a quick whisper within a dream or an afterthought post orgasm. Slowly it grew louder until her mind was consumed completely. It was always with her now. Lived inside her in a place no penis could reach. Deeper than any man could go.

Miyako felt guilty. She possessed the love of all of her men. She had more money than she could ever need. A home of her own. Beautiful things to herself. A fabulous wardrobe. A life she filled with everything to please herself.

Shouldn't that be enough for her? Couldn't all her desires be fulfilled through the means already at her disposal?

These attempts at reasoning couldn't quench her hunger.

Naked to her own primal thoughts but afraid of her own longing, Miyako continued her futile attempts to fight it off. Not because it was something too taboo or kinky, she loved riding on the edge of sexual deviancy, but because it was something foreign to her entirely. Something she didn't quite understand about herself. The truth would open doors to places inside her, she wasn't sure she could handle where they'd lead. Certainly, no man could reach this part of her either. That scared her even more.

One day when she was alone in her apartment in bed and found herself too distracted to masturbate, she came clean to herself. She wanted something more for herself.

She felt the fear in admitting this, but relief at the same time. She freed herself by facing her desire. Before, Miyako thought she learned everything about herself through her line of work. But there was still so much to find. Her mind was a large space, galaxies beyond what her own body could provide in exploration. Vast unknowns were inside her, and it was unlikely she'd ever discovered everything she contained. She knew she had to honor that. But she also needed to honor the truths, which did surface. That meant also being honest about this new truth she learned about herself. What dormant need had been awakened over the years. Despite what the soldiers gave her, it all made her long for something they couldn't give her.

Because it was a man she searched for.

A man perfected by war.

Who loved deeply but was proficient at the art of combat. Who fought better than anyone, as a result, of natural talent and dedication to fighting. Yet chose to preserve life at all cost.

Was such a thing possible? Miyako chose to believe so. She couldn't love a man who loved to kill. Life was something to be enjoyed and treasured. There was pleasure to the simple act of being alive. She hated how lives had been cut short due to war. Despite the anger in her heart at those who'd extended the fighting, she didn't want anyone else to die, especially, not in the ways war took lives.

She wanted a war hero and peace walker. A man with long dark wild hair. A man with blue eyes with depths to another world. Beyond the blue of the American flag that alluded to Miyako's beloved night or the lipstick she wore. Blue of another meaning entirely known only by a powerful presence beyond. A serious man who focused on the mission at hand. A man who only spoke with wise and loving words even if it meant he spoke less than others. What he did in life spoke for him. He'd have a huge presence because of who he was, not because he cared how others saw him. He simply did what was needed and what was right. A man who lived in the moment because he couldn't be any other way. A man who survived horrors of war beyond what anyone else encountered. Yet survived while keeping his true self intact.

Miyako could love this kind of man beyond anything she ever felt before.

Yet, Miyako wasn't sure such a man could love her. She wasn't sure if she deserved such a wonderful man. But she knew she wanted him more than anything.

Where would she find such a man?

Could such a man exist?

Miyako wondered if she'd face a lifetime searching for the impossible or the pain of loving someone who would never love her back.

She'd fought hard to hide from her ultimate desire and considering the grim realities of her dream, she understood why.

***

Shinju showed up at Miyako's door and woke Miyako up with her usual loud banging and yelling. She said she needed the money from this one client, but he was bringing a friend and would refuse her if she didn't bring a date.

Miyako shrugged, quickly dressed, and followed Shinju out the door.

Shinju took her to a new food joint Miyako hadn't been to before. Waiting for them were two fairly young soldiers.

"Here's your date for your virgin!" Shinju called while holding up Miyako's arm

"Hey!" cried one of the men. "You weren't supposed to say anything about that!"

Shinju stuck out her tongue.

"Fuck man," the other man punched the other in the arm. "Why did you go telling her that?"

Upon sitting down in the restaurant booth and starting a conversation with the men, learning the blond virgin was George, and John was the other guy, Miyako learned neither had any combat experience as Shinju embarrassingly forced the men to admit.

"Don't worry, all American soldiers are sexy!" Miyako replied.

She knew she wasn't going to sleep with either of them. She would ensure she would never see them again. Still, she'd enjoy the date as much as she could. Especially, the extra time with Shinju, which was becoming scarce.

When the food arrived, John pulled out a red bottle seemingly from thin air. Shinju immediately attempted to snatch the bottle.

"Easy girl," he said. "You don't want to chug this. But it will add some zing to your culinary experience."

"You sure it's okay?" George asked.

"These kinds of girls can handle it. They aren't our prissy girls from back home. These ladies are tough," John said. "Ready to try some Tabasco?" He looked to Miyako.

"Tabasco." Miyako slowly uttered the syllables. They tickled her lips. "Yes, I'd love to try some."

This date was proving to be interesting after all. Even if these weren't American heroes. Even if she wouldn't fall in love this time.

John poured red liquid on Miyako's open burger and spilled some on the side of her fries. It reminded Miyako of Ketchup, but the way the liquid moved was different. It reflected the light as if it were a red ocean. Miyako eagerly wolfed her burger and fries. The spice on her lips tantalized her. She continued eating.

"I see you like it," he said. "You want some on your food, Sin?"

Shinju took a tiny dip with a fry into Miyako's drying red puddle on her plate.

"Hey, that's mine!" Miyako said. She already loved this stuff.

Shinju's face contorted at the taste and she quickly spit it out. Cursing wildly until John ordered her to stop.

Miyako eagerly took the bottle in front of John's plate and drowned her food in it.

"Where can I get more of this?" Miyako asked.

John laughed, "Just keep that bottle. I'm sure you'll find more. Glad you like it."

Shinju scowled for the rest of the date. Taking refuge in frequent sips of water and quieter cursing.

***

After that, Miyako always carried at least one small bottle of Tabasco in her purse. She bought crates of it in stores, and her lovers would gift her bottles of the red sauce. Red like fire, sex, passion, and love. Miyako thought such a condiment fit her lifestyle perfectly. Miyako's newfound love of Tabasco became a source of cruel jokes from Shinju, but the men seemed to get a kick out of it. She'd even replaced cigarettes for Tabasco. The liquid brought life to her mouth completely beating out her failed routine of smoking.

***

Miyako was amazed by how closely related sex and food were. And it wasn't just because many of her meals were closely followed by sex. The parts of the body for food consumption and processing were the same areas used in sex. Both food and sex enticed all the senses. Miyako realized this as a lover fed her chocolates as she lay before him in bed. It was what the Americans called Valentine's Day. She was his Valentine and enjoyed the assortment of chocolates her lover received in the mail from his girlfriend. She'd forgotten both of their names from all the pink wine she'd drank. A few hours later, she would be another man's Valentine. Then another's. Blessed with the pleasures of eating and lovemaking, Miyako couldn't think of a better American holiday. Hot sauce surprisingly went well with Valentine's chocolates.

***

After a date with Sam, Miyako chose to go home alone. His bed hadn't been big enough for the two of them and his snoring would make her unable to sleep despite her heavy drinking that night. She wouldn't be seeing him again. Nothing romantic or sexual had occurred, leaving Miyako feeling as if she'd wasted her night.

Miyako sipped on a little of Tabasco along the way to get the taste of alcohol out of her mouth and kill the smell on her breath. Tabasco proved to have many uses.

Miyako judgment was still cloudy by cream and vodka as she walked home. She was drifting into her fantasy world and dreaming about her perfect soldier. Envisioning a scene, he'd survive in the war. Conjured an epic rescue of a beautiful woman in the midst of it all.

She wasn't sure when the man appeared in front of her on the road. Miyako paused when she felt his presence. She admired his handsome body, despite not fitting her exact tastes. His features were incredibly sharp. Yet, something inside her kept her from drawing closer or speaking.

The man smiled. That's when Miyako noticed the fox eyes. Black and bottomless. She was dealing with a Kitsune. In front of her very eyes, he transformed into the mental image of the man who she'd been dreaming of. She felt violated. How could he know such details? Yet, she found herself approaching her dream soldier in the darkness, wanting to see how his blue eyes would glimmer in the night. Then the man turned into a fox and ran off into the shadows of the trees.

***

Miyako suspected Shinju trained for work in Gion. Whether she'd been a Geisha or not, Miyako wasn't sure. Shinju was never going to tell her. The war made that line of work difficult to maintain. Women were only returning to it with Americans around and money flowing again. It was possible Shinju left due to her need for money and decided even now her lifestyle simply paid her more than being a Geisha ever could.

Miyako overheard some women calling themselves Geishas in order to get American clients though Miyako knew from their mannerisms they definitely weren't. While Miyako didn't care about the misrepresentation of her Japan, her men already ruined that for her, it did annoy her somehow. She was the exotic one, not them. Geishas were exotic beyond what she could be. Another pretending to be one turned her blood to ice.

Yet, she did nothing to defend the Geisha.

While taking an alternative route to avoid an impending police raid, Miyako and Shinju encountered a Geisha. She was petite and beautiful. What she wore only accentuated this. It was an equally beautiful kimono. Black veined with pink cherry blossoms blooming abundantly over delicate wood branches. Exactly the kind of kimono Miyako would have wanted for herself.

The Geisha looked lost and confused. Whoever was supposed to be accompanying her wasn't there.

"What? You stick your nose at us? You think you're better than us?"

The Geisha looked as confused as ever. Shinju suddenly was creating a confrontation from thin air. This wasn't typical even of the obnoxious Shinju.

"Look at me," Shinju ordered.

The Geisha attempted to flee.

Shinju grabbed her by the arms. The Geisha cried in pain.

"Look at me. Look me in the eyes and tell me you're better than me. Say it to my face." Shinju pressed the woman into a wall.

The Geisha looked Shinju in the eyes. Miyako saw pools of tears ready to flow into rivers.

"Come on. Let her go," Miyako said.

"Not until I'm finished." Shinju only lowered her pitch at the last word when it was clear she realized she'd been screaming.

Shinju slapped the Geisha. Then she started undressing the woman violently breathing as if she'd been left out in the cold too long. Miyako stood by and watched in shock. The woman frozen, silenced by fear. Shinju ran her hands over exposed skin and the woman's breast still shielded by fabric.

Shinju went to tear off the rest of her kimono. Miyako placed her hands over Shinju's.

"No." Miyako's voice quiet but firm.

A kimono was a reflection of the Geisha as an artist, an individual, and as a soul. Miyako wasn't going to let it be destroyed.

Shinju spat at the girl and flung Miyako's hands away. Shinju took off running and Miyako followed.

Miyako looked back and saw her escort had finally found her as the Geisha remained sobbing in the street. He was already helping her put the rest of her clothes back on. The Geisha locked eyes with her until Miyako turned back and quickened her pace.

Despite the Geisha's temporary misfortune, Miyako couldn't help but wish she was her.

***

Miyako waited two hours until it became clear her date wasn't going to show. This was a first for her. She didn't speculate why he hadn't come, but let the emotions of disappointment take over. She at least took solace in not wasting any of her blue lipstick on him. She'd accidentally left it at home while switching purses. She'd wanted her lover to see her use the purse he gifted her several weeks before on their date. But it didn't match the dress she longed to wear in the night for the other man.

Miyako left the bar and waited in front of a movie theater for another potential client to show. All the men already with a beautiful woman in tow. No lovers for her tonight. Miyako screeched and kicked the building. Then she took a breath and went inside.

She angrily chewed on her popcorn as she watched the steamy romance, sexual frustration building like a volcano. Each romantic scene was fueled the lust within her. She loudly slurped her soda, wishing it was a dick. A few couples eyed her through the darkness. A staring contest ensued in which Miyako always won. Not a word was spoken to her.

Miyako left while the theater was still dark. She'd already seen this movie six times anyway. She stomped as she walked her way home. Tears threatened to make rivers on her face. She'd failed to be a lover of the Americans tonight. Defeated by other women.

Rustling of leaves accented the click of footsteps. Miyako was being followed. She turned and hooked her fist into the stomach of the man behind her. He crumbled. Miyako did some more moves a lover taught her for her own protection.

A Japanese man lay on the ground. She kicked him continually as laughter escaped her mouth. He wasn't going to be getting up anytime soon. Miyako felt pleased.

"Trying to rape me, you little bitch? Because the Americans can have me and you can't?"

"Such a beautiful woman you are. You're disgracing yourself with foreign blood." The man spoke slowly.

"You failed us!" She sneered. Her anger building even more. "You failed us and we lost everything, and you wanted to take more?"

"What are you talking about? I just wanted to talk to you. I have for some time. But you won't even acknowledge me. It's as if Japanese men don't exist to you."

Miyako had never seen him before.

"You're right, you don't exist to me. No Japanese man does. It's just what you all deserve. The Americans were always smarter and better. And guess what? They know how to please in bed! You're the disgrace, not me! You're not worthy of me. You never were! That's why you kept me down so I would never realize how pathetic you were! I know how to be independent from you now! I have money and a home all for myself! The men failed us and other men came along so I could be free."

"Fool, you're not independent. I see what you do. You're tools for the Americans!"

"In terms of economy, yes I am! You couldn't care for us! Not financially and not emotionally. You never showed us women any love. None at all. Yet we were expected to serve you. Well, you lost the war. Thank you for that at least, it revealed how pathetic you all really are. I have a new master now. Myself! I have money and my own home. I only do what I want. No more cooking and serving tea. Such a boring life you want your woman to have. Just so we would never realize how pitiful you really are. No Japanese man would ever let me seek my own pleasure. Forget about ever orgasming to whatever you humped out in the bedroom. I bet you finish in thirty seconds. Never pleasing a woman, you pathetic man. And I choose to serve men with bigger cocks! Cocks a real woman can orgasm to. Americans are the real men!"

The man tried to get up but Miyako kicked him again, smiling at her own words. The man tried to rise once more but fell to the ground and sobbed. Reeking of alcohol, he cried so hard, he threw up. A useless drunk. A woman who could still serve just a man was stupid. Miyako would never feel bad for such a woman again. The man continued to cry.

Miyako kicked him in the stomach and told him to die for his honor. Just like Japan wanted him too. She ran into the night and let herself disappear into it. She made it home without any other incident, besides catching a mysterious wisp of a gray fox.

***

Miyako jumped into bed. She considered what to do for the rest of her night. She wasn't in the mood for one of her American hobbies. She decided to masturbate instead.

She started touching herself as the soldiers taught her to. She imagined all the sexiest parts from every guy and all the hottest things they'd ever done. She felt herself swell and bloom.

Then she thought of her dream soldier. Moments later, she climaxed and collapsed into bliss before falling asleep.

She dreamed of her American soldier. She approached, embracing him. He evaporated before her eyes. What was left behind was a cold and empty space that stretched on forever.

The dream was disturbing, and Miyako decided to take the day off.

***

The spring brought pink blooms of cherry blossoms. This was the time of year Miyako's old superstitious of spirits came back to her. Hidden among the trees and invisibly floating in the air, their presence couldn't be denied while their intentions remained a mystery. Were they watching? What dramas occurred in their realm? Did tragedy ever touch them? Was joy in their experience? What strings did they pull in the life of humans? These unknowns frustrated and scared Miyako.

Miyako wanted to be a cherry blossom when she was a little girl. She thought the ideal woman was like a cherry blossom, beautiful and delicate but connected the elements of each passing year. It captured attention without extreme measures, by remaining itself. These flowers bloomed for their own sake, not for the sake of others.

Even the Geisha who danced during this time of year, did so more for themselves than others. Miyako realized this as she watched them. They smiled and glowed as they moved within the current of the instruments. Miyako wondered if her ex-lover Drew would appreciate it all. She knew Roger would as he stood watching.

She reminded herself not to follow suite with Shinju too much. Shinju lost her feminine delicacy. Her inner beauty was fading with each passing day. Shinju was losing herself and it made Miyako sad. She was unable to help her. Perhaps ones of the Americans would save her. She was surprised that hadn't happened already.

It was better to be like the cherry blossom, reborn again and again in life. Bloom when the time was right. nature's orgasm.

Miyako returned to the apartment alone. The cluttered made her feel sick. She started to clean. She didn't need to do anymore shopping. It didn't matter there were savings under the bed. She was growing greedy. She wanted to appreciate each gift for what it was. She threw out clothes that she had stopped wearing due to wear or changes in taste. She kept all her stuffed animals but put them neatly on the tables or her bed.

Be like a cherry blossom, Miyako told herself.

***

Another late morning slumber was interrupted by Shinju's banging at Miyako's door. Shinju once again said she needed Miyako for another double date. Miyako was furious. She'd been dreaming of her ideal soldier again, and sleep was the only way she could see him. She'd finally been communing with him in the dream world. Miyako wanted to tell Shinju off, tell her how angry she was for interrupting her dream just so she could use Miyako's body to make money. Shinju told Miyako to meet her at the new bar that night and walked off before Miyako had a chance to yell at her. Telling Shinju about her dream would have been stupid, Miyako surmised. Shinju didn't care about using Miyako. Why would saying anything about a dream matter?

Miyako considered flaking out on Shinju, but she wanted the chance to meet more American heroes. Worst-case scenario, she would ditch them and go find what she desired elsewhere. Shinju never actually got mad when she bailed.

The two men Shinju picked as clients were handsome enough for Miyako's taste. They offered Miyako drinks but didn't force her to take down too much. She leisurely sipped a glass of pink liquid as the three discussed American cuisine. Shinju took shot after shot. She was drinking more heavily than usual, and that was a feat for Shinju. Afterward they followed the two men back to a hotel. Miyako felt either man was worthy of at least a blow job.

Miyako noticed Shinju was watching her as they went back to the hotel.

In the room, one of the men asked if the two women were interested in a card game. Shinju said no. Miyako feared the look in Shinju's eyes.

Shinju pounced on Miyako and kissed her, forcing her tongue into her mouth. Miyako didn't respond at first. She was slow to process what was happening. Shinju stripped Miyako of her clothes so fast she wasn't aware it was happening until she was already naked in front of all three of them. Miyako wasn't sure why this was happening. Was it the alcohol? Some deeper lust finally emerging? Did the men care? But they didn't intervene.

Shinju ordered Miyako to lay on the bed. Miyako obeyed. She opened her legs and kept her hands to her sides. Shinju took off her own clothes as quickly. From the bed, Miyako admired Shinju's pale body. All over, she had white winter skin of the Yuki-Onni. It made her eyes and hair glimmered like the ocean at night. Miyako wondered how a woman like her could possibly be mortal. She was indeed shapely, her clothes had been honest to the world about that. Her breasts were like beautiful ivory orbs. But there were scars all over the rest of her body. Burns, cuts, scratches, bruises, and bites. Shinju went through so much and continued to survive. She was a product of war and pain too. Shinju jumped onto Miyako, aligning herself to touch as much of Miyako's sensitive places as possible. Shinju looked into Miyako's eyes.

"You're beautiful," Miyako told Shinju as she looked back. Shinju silenced her by diving deeply into her, anywhere she could.

Their flowering parts were touching. It felt so natural. Women could make love to each other after all. Would she finally get to orgasm to the feel of a woman? It was as if Miyako been on a verge of receiving an orgasm from Shinju for years, only now getting the hope for a final and ultimate release. Shinju's moved her mouth and tongue over Miyako's lips and breasts. Miyako reciprocated.

Shinju went about taking Miyako differently. She bit her neck and nipples at times, bringing a loud moan out of Miyako. This caused Shinju to work more intensely into Miyako. Finally, Shinju started to kiss a line from Miyako's lips, to each breast, down her stomach, and to her thighs. Miyako was at first disappointed Shinju skipped her blooming parts. But just as quickly Shinju was kissing the top of her vagina and plunged her tongue into the inside part of her flowering parts.

Miyako orgasmed three times for Shinju consecutively as Shinju instantly moved her lips along her there, occasionally forcing her tongue into her tunnel. Miyako fell into a state of bliss.

When Shinju finished, she lifted off of Miyako. Then one of the already naked men, except for a condom, was upon Miyako and was instantly inside of her when he touched the bed. Miyako forgotten about the two men until then. But she was ready for a man's touch again.

She finally shared another world with Shinju, so many curiosities clarified and put to rest. Having already been satisfied so well, Miyako gave herself fully not expecting any pleasure in return. But she orgasmed for the man too. Again and again until he came inside of her as well.

Miyako fell asleep.

When she awoke it was morning. Shinju was still naked, legs splayed and vagina open. Miyako wanted to surprise her with an orgasm. Still naked herself, she approached Shinju on the bed. She knelt beside her and put her mouth to her pussy gently kissing her there. Shinju made delightful noises with her eyes still closed. Her vagina was blooming for Miyako, and she was pleased. Miyako learned a vagina tasted different than a penis. Wetter and sweeter. Women really were gentle, sweet, and beautiful inside. Shinju started to shake and Miyako pushed some more, hoping this was a sign for an oncoming orgasm in her as it was for Miyako. Suddenly she felt a rush of air, and a cry come from Shinju's lips. A burst of energy from her flower.

Miyako had finally done it. She had experienced the whole package of making love to a woman.

Shinju looked down at Miyako, only now opening her eyes. But suddenly Shinju started screaming.

"You bitch!" She rose up and tired to slap Miyako. The men awoke quickly to break the two apart, still naked themselves.

"Why would you do that to me?"

"What about last night?"

"They offered me a lot of money to watch me with a girl! That's why I did it. I hated it the whole time."

"We wouldn't have paid you if you didn't want to do it. We didn't mean to make you do something you didn't want to," the taller one said this. Miyako didn't remember either of their names.

"Shut up! All men are liars! You let her rape me."

Miyako started crying. "Shinju, I'm so sorry. It was just that you said you'd never had an orgasm and after last night I…"

Shinju spit in Miyako's face. Shinju hurriedly got dressed and left. Both men stayed and comforted a sobbing Miyako.

"We're really sorry. We just mentioned in passing we'd never saw two girls do it before and we asked if she knew anyone who would be interested. We didn't mean for any of this to happen. Is your friend going to be okay?" the taller one asked.

"I don't know. I think she hates me. I think she only uses me to make money."

"Well I don't think women can actually rape, so you should be okay," the shorter one said.

"That's not the right thing to say. But truthfully, this whole thing was Shinju's idea. She offered to have sex with a girl in front of us before we mentioned anything to her."

Was Shinju that desperate for clients?

They took Miyako out for breakfast, barely talked about anything at all while only eating small amounts. Miyako went home after and took a nap. She didn't have to worry about any repeat clients for another day and a half. By then, she hoped she would be in the mood to fuck again.

Shinju arrived at Miyako's apartment later to apologize. She admitted the idea was hers and she'd gotten a huge advance for the promise of having sex with a woman in their presence. Shinju was ready to split the money with Miyako, but she didn't have the heart to take it. Shinju told Miyako they would never touch again, even for the pleasure of a client. Miyako nodded. She was done with women anyway. In the end, she preferred men much more. Shinju agreed she would come by when she needed her for double dates. Miyako nodded to this too. As Shinju turned to leave, Miyako couldn't help but ask.

"You sure you're okay, Shinju?"

Shinju was silent for a while before exhaling loudly and answering, "The problem wasn't that I didn't enjoy it. The problem was that I did."

She left before Miyako could say another word.

**

Miyako didn't see Shinju for two weeks. Then Shinju showed up at Miyako's door and asked her again to meet for a double date at a local bar. Miyako didn't ask if Shinju got that advance. It would have been easy to disappear without providing the service she'd promised. Something didn't add up.

That night, during the date, Miyako noticed Shinju acting strangely. She was sitting at the bar and barely acknowledged Miyako or either client. She was jittery like a cold sparrow, her eyes flying about. Her eyelids occasionally fluttered, drawing attention to their redness matching her lipstick. Miyako struggled to hear or understand what she was saying. Miyako wondered if Shinju was already drunk when she reached the bar, since she arrived late. Still, Shinju never acted like this when she was drunk before. After several shots, she'd normally be shouting and describing sexual favors she was willing to provide. She'd certainly never been quiet after drinking.

When one of the men put his hand on Shinju's shoulder, she jolted. The man shook his head and left with his friend. Miyako followed them outside and apologized. In a local alley, she fucked them both before returning to the bar. Shinju didn't seem to notice.

"Shinju, the clients are gone. You're not in the condition tonight for this. Go home and sleep," Miyako said.

Shinju didn't move or acknowledge her. After several attempts to rouse her, Shinju was still not responding. Miyako gently pulled her off of her chair. She draped Shinju around her arm and dragged her out of the bar and back to her apartment. After searching Shinju for several minutes outside the door, Miyako found Shinju's keys tucked into her underwear. Opening the door unleashed a smell of decay and rot. Miyako didn't hide her sounds of repulsion. She considered bringing Shinju back to her own place, but ultimately placed Shinju on her own bed. Miyako laid Shinju on her side and heard Shinju moan, but not much else. Miyako left.

A few days later, Shinju showed up at Miyako's place and asked her to meet up for a double date at the same location. She never acknowledged what happened the other night. Miyako agreed, but felt wary. This time, the men never showed up.

After leaving the bar, Shinju pulled out a gun she'd been hiding in her purse. She explained she started carrying it after one of the men gave it to her as a gift. Miyako suspected otherwise but couldn't bring herself to inquire her.

The gun made Miyako feel afraid. She never felt fear of the guns her lovers carried. She thought little of them besides the occasional feeling of extra protection. This was different. Shinju seemed on edge with her gun, she didn't understand what she was carrying. She wasn't in the right mind to handle its power to kill.

"You have to protect yourself from everything. You can't trust these men," Shinju said before hiding her gun away in her purse once again.

Miyako didn't think she could handle any more double dates with Shinju. She decided she would stop joining her for now. She wouldn't respond to Shinju knocking at her door anymore. Even if her schedule was free.

Miyako wondered if she was somehow responsible for Shinju's odd behavior or if she cracked due to some of the horrible men she worked for. It hurt her to think she might have hurt Shinju or if she hadn't stopped someone else from doing so. Still, she was now afraid of Shinju, and didn't feel like she could do anything for her now. Miyako cried herself to sleep over it for three nights.

***

Occasionally, Miyako would deal with what was called break-ups. A lot of times they weren't necessary because the men would let her know when they'd be leaving. Miyako understood when her lovers had to return to their wives and girlfriends. Sometimes all they had to return to was their country, and this made Miyako sad. She wanted her lovers to continue having love even after they left her. She knew she held a special place in her lover's hearts.

She'd never truly leave them and they'd never leave her.

Any sadness she felt went away when she reminded herself there were always plenty of new and exciting men to love. Better to appreciate a love fresh and in season then to ponder upon a romance that withered away.

There was the occasional man who would reappear after a few months, but that was rare. Often, Miyako would have lost interest by that point. While an out of season fruit could be exciting at the moment, it felt out of place quickly. Miyako would release these men shortly to take their needs elsewhere. The guys she loved the most seemed to stick around for a long time. Some loves stay in season all year long.

But when break-ups occurred, Miyako found them awkward and unnecessary. Often she would just laugh and leave with a hastened good-bye. Whatever would get her out of the situation the fastest so she could move back to fruitful romances,

One man made things particularly weird. Miyako ignored her gut upon meeting a guy out in a garden, she wanted to try a redhead, and slept with him. They'd been out to burgers with each other for a few weeks. Lenny was across the table, fidgeting and sighing. Miyako was annoyed but did her best to play the situation as coolly as she could. After all, she was a cool girl who had to stay cool at times. Miyako was slurping on a coke with cherry syrup when Lenny broke the silence.

"Hey, we need to talk."

"Yeah. This no talking is freaking me out. It's like a horror movie."

"Well, you're not going to be happy, but we can't see each other anymore."

"Okay." Miyako cheerfully continued sipping on her coke.

"Okay…like okay or?"

"Okay."

"You don't need a reason or anything? I just feel bad about cheating on my wife and…."

"Why? You even said I did that thing your wife didn't do. It's natural you would want…"

"It's against my religion and I'm a father of two and…" He interrupted.

"Stop. It's fine."

"Really? I just didn't want you getting attached. You seemed to really like me."

"Not really."

"Are you just saying that because you're upset?"

"Nope."

"Well, I just want you to know that…"

"Really, it's fine. Your penis is too small anyway and you're not exciting in bed. I have plenty of men who please me. You're terrible at getting me to orgasm. You only last a few seconds. I feel bad for your wife if you have sex with her the same way. She can't be happy with you." She folded her hands under her chin and smiled.

Lenny slapped her payment on the table and left, right before their burgers arrived. Miyako was so hungry she ended up eating both, adding another coke with cherry syrup. She vowed to never again ignore her gut on a man for the sake of trying someone seemingly exotic or to escape a night of boredom.

Her mind then wandered back to her meal before she plotted her evening with Roger. He'd make up for the organisms Lenny failed to provide.

***

Shinju banged on Miyako's door every day for a month until Miyako finally answered. Based on Miyako's gut, she decided to join Shinju for a night at the movies. Shinju's color had returned and her new dress sleekly rode her body's curves. Perhaps it was a sign Shinju was on the mend. Miyako didn't have any other clients to attend to that night.

Shinju took Miyako to a part of the city they'd never worked in before. Shinju told Miyako a police raid was going on in their own turf. Shinju managed to hang on to her cop client it appeared.

But during their walk, Shinju repeatedly told Miyako about her policeman's small dick and how she'd never date such a man again.

They passed a brothel. Shinju told Miyako not to make eye contact with anyone and look only at the road in front. Miyako felt something terrible as they walked by. The sounds she heard coming from inside made her shudder. There were moans, but not the ones of pleasure or longing. But it wasn't the sounds that captured Miyako's full attention. It was the smell.

The smell Miyako would catch from her lovers when they awoke and screamed in the night. It hadn't happened too many times as she was the one who usually woke up sweaty, terrified, but the smell on them was identical to hers. Based on their panting and the few words that escaped them before and after awakening, Miyako knew it was combat related.

The smell reaching out from that place confirmed the personal scars of war. Wars of the men and women mingling together. Battles they now each faced alone despite their shared fates. Committing sexual acts, making the smell stronger. Instead of escape, sex amplified the pain of their war. Miyako was growing faint. Shinju grabbed Miyako's arm to steady her.

A few moments later, Shinju told Miyako it was safe to look up again.

But it wasn't.

Miyako saw two girls dressed like lifeless dolls. She could only see their backs from where she walked with Shinju. Too young to be as dirty as they were. They were walking hand in hand and looked straight ahead. Shinju grabbed Miyako and pulled her ahead of them, stepping around them so their hands remained intact. Miyako looked behind and Shinju jerked her forward. She wanted to see their faces. Miyako looked back and thought their eyes looked black at first. But they weren't. They were muddy. They were swamps that pulled her in and suffocated her. What girls could live having such eyes? She wanted to help heal them. Bring them to the Americans to fix their eyes. Her Americans could fix this, they've already been fixing the rest of Japan.

She wanted to call out to them, give them hope. Give them a chance to be loved by someone. But she continued looking at them without uttering a word. Her mouth opened as wide as her eyes, but no sound emerged. Shinju jabbed her thumb into Miyako's side, which made Miyako look down as she yelped. Then she looked into Shinju's eyes. Miyako never noticed how dark her eyes were before. Perhaps they only become so at that moment, or Miyako was finally seeing something she hadn't before. The same pits were there too. But hers went even deeper. Shinju pushed Miyako forward faster until the girls were out of sight.

Miyako knew what she wanted to say to Shinju, but she decided to wait until after their dates.

Which never happened. The two couldn't find any clients that night, so they caught a movie together instead. It was some action flick that Shinju kept laughing and filling the theatre with her sounds and echoes.

But she wasn't laughing her usual laugh. Miyako could hear Shinju pushing the sounds out of her throat with force. Each laugh came with difficulty, and at the wrong times for the plot. Miyako looked to her popcorn as if it could gently tell her what she already knew, Shinju wasn't getting better. She stared at the kernels joyfully arranged in the bucket as her only solace.

After the lights came back on, Shinju got up and Miyako bolted up and dashed in order to not lose sight of her. On the walk back to their turf, Shinju lead Miyako a different way that didn't pass the brothel. A back way near a garden and a river.

"Why are you avoiding that place, Shinju?" Miyako heard the words before she realized she said them.

"It smells bad," retorted Shinju.

"I know that's not the reason, Shinju." Again, Miyako heard the words before she knew the thought.

"Stop saying my name like that!"

"Did you know that place? Did you work there?" Miyako was building her courage.

"Absolutely not!" Shinju scowled as if a scary face could keep Miyako's words at bay.

Yet, the truth was clear. Shinju had been there. Her eyes betrayed her lie.

"Shinju, it doesn't matter…"

"To hell it doesn't!"

"You mean so much to me, Shinju. Please, none of that matters to me. You're the same to me."

"Hah! You care about me? Now, I know you have a screw loose."

"I'm serious, Shinju!"

"Stop saying my name, Miyako!"

"Just talk to me!"

"How is an ex-Geisha supposed to feel about a girl from a brothel?"

"I wasn't a Geisha."

"You were training to be one. Close enough."

"I never got that far. It doesn't matter."

"It does. And you being stupid makes that hurt more."

The conversation was interrupted by the sounds of splashing. Both women turned to see a girl on a bridge looking down into the disturbed water far below. In horror, Miyako realized it was one of the girls from earlier that night. The other jumped into the water already.

Before she knew it, Miyako was running toward the girl, alluding Shinju's grasp to stop her before she felt her on her skin. Miyako found her voice for the remaining girl.

"Stop, please!"

The girl looked at her with her muddy eyes. The moment lasted for a lifetime. Miyako was lost in her eyes as the girl plummeted to her death below.

"No!" Miyako screamed.

She looked to the water and fell to her knees crying. Miyako could swim. But the girls dropped from such a height, she knew they were dead. She stayed like that until Shinju approached her.

"Why didn't you try to stop them?" Miyako nearly choked on her own words.

"If they wanted to be dead, there's good reason. A lot of the girls in that line of work get sick from all the sex."

"Isn't that what condoms are for?"

"Condoms aren't used in the whorehouse."

"Why?"

"People in these kinds of places don't care to use them. They use and discard each other equally. And themselves."

Miyako looked at the water. She didn't see the bodies. They were already swept under a powerful current.

"That, or they were just unhappy."

"Did you know them?"

Shinju paused.

"You did, didn't you?"

Shinju started to walk away from Miyako with her back turned.

"You could have brought them to our life. You could have saved them. They would have been safe with the Americans."

"Stop it, Miyako."

"That could have been me, Shinju. If you hadn't found me, I could have been dying off that bridge. Why save me and not them?"

Shinju continued to walk away.

"Answer me, Shinju!"

"Maybe you were just at the right place at the right time. I don't know. Especially with how much you're pissing me off right now."

She walked a little and then added. "Some of my clients were skittish meeting up with me alone. I needed a partner. Someone cute and unthreatening. I saw how scared and desperate you were. I knew you wouldn't say no. You secured my job and my money. That's all you've ever been to me."

Shinju left Miyako there. It took Miyako another hour until she found the strength in her legs to leave.

***

Shinju didn't come back to Miyako's apartment. Miyako didn't need her help anymore. She hadn't in a long time. But she needed her help once, when she came off the train all those years ago. Otherwise, she would have likely ended up at the brothel too.

Why did Shinju save her from such a life? From the very one she suffered? The one caused by the war. Besides sex, what other choices in making a living did they have when war made everything else so difficult?

Miyako's new life was just another cage.

Miyako took a few days off from work. She knew when she returned to the Americans they would help her forget. Even if only temporarily. Pain was fleeting as was remembering and forgetting. Pleasure took that all away.

Miyako stayed in bed with a man a whole day. John. Each time he entered her, he seemed to be losing himself in her as she was in him. Miyako wondered what he was trying to forget. She wondered if he was struggling to remember pleasure and love, or if he was feeling them genuinely with her. She never orgasmed so many times in one day with one man.

When they'd finished, he smoked a cigarette next to Miyako and told her it was the best sex he ever had. She smiled and stroked his chest.

Miyako waited for him to tell her what had been on his mind, but he fell asleep. When they awoke the next morning, all he asked was if she was available next Thursday.

He left without telling her anything more.

How well did she know him? Despite all their conversations, despite him being inside her, despite all that time together, how much did she really know him? Even the sex this time showed her something else about him. But it left her with more mystery than answers. Like Shinju, there were things she didn't know about the men she thought to know so well. Could she ever fully know someone inside and out? Could she ever know someone's entire being? Would everyone always have secrets locked away? Even the perfect soldier she dreamed of?

Upon second thought, Miyako thought it might have been hypocritical to think these people were not opening up to her enough. She hid secrets too. She hadn't told them about the family she abandoned, but only after, they abandoned her first. She didn't tell any of her favorite clients about each other. She never revealed who had the biggest dick (Harry), who made her orgasm the most (John), who was her favorite man to kiss or to make love to not love too (Roger). Which man had her favorite laugh (Drew), which man gave her the best presents and hugs (Andrew). Could they ever know and fully understand her when she wouldn't reveal such intimate details about herself? Even if it hurt? Killed the romance? Was that the price? Certainly, that wasn't something Miyako was willing to give up.

Why did she expect them to reveal such details about themselves?

Did she want to hear if an American lover was better than she could ever be? That she wasn't what they would consider wife material? How many girls they loved more than her? The woman they saw in their dreams at night? Or whose face they saw when they closed their eyes? Did she want to hear more war stories when she already learned too much from her lovers on drunken nights? When she was already having more and more nightmares as time went on?

How many of the men would keep her unspoken secret after they returned to America? Would they ever look at their ceilings or skies at night to think of Miyako? And what would they say if their wives and girlfriends asked what they were thinking, would they say nothing? Or would they be silent, as Miyako had with her men when she'd think of her dream soldier, and just know there were secrets they could never really know? Their women had secrets, perhaps in love too.

Perhaps it was more important to share their time together in intimacy, which only went so deep. Or perhaps intimacy where despite the mystery, the connection remained. It was still real, even if all the details weren't revealed. The connection mattered more.

When Miyako returned to John on schedule, she gave herself physically as fully as she could. She loved him, all of him, even the parts she didn't know. She loved his body and his mystery. She loved him despite not knowing him because in doing so she still knew him fully. There was something that went deeper between lovers even if certain words were never spoken.

When they'd finished and John fell asleep, Miyako stared out the window into the night sky. She longed for her dream soldier more each passing day. She hoped she could share something even deeper with him. Know him fully. Every story, even the mundane ones. Even the dark and gory ones. Even his moments of failure. She wanted to know one person like that. Him.

She wanted someone to know her life fully too. She wanted a man with whom she could share mutual courage in being fully exposed and still being loved for it. Still, she wondered if such a man could truly love her. The same man she wanted to love. Many times her own dreams told her otherwise.

***

After a particularly romantic lunch date, despite the lack of sex, Miyako walked back to her apartment. Sometimes, being romanced by a man was more than enough. Her head was in the clouds and she was startled to see Andrew at her doorway. She hadn't been expecting him for another few hours. But he was also her last client for the day. Still it was strange because he never showed up early, in fact, he tended to run a bit late.

"Hey," he said. "Can we talk?"

Was this going to be one of those awkward break-ups? Miyako hoped not, but his facial express showed something serious. She liked him, she hoped they could have sex at least one last time. But she wouldn't beg for him, she had her pride and plenty of other men to sleep with.

She opened the door and Andrew followed her inside. He sat down with her on the bed. Miyako waited, expecting bad news.

"I have something for you," Andrew said.

Miyako sighed in relief. No break-ups tonight! She would definitely be getting laid. A present too! She grinned extra wide so Andrew could see. The men only built up their presents if it was something good. It must be extremely expensive or rare. Miyako grew excited. Andrew had good taste, which was apparent in his previous present giving. To date, he was the man who spent the most on her. He given her necklaces with so many diamonds her neck twinkled like a star. Shoes so pretty Miyako only wore them when she was alone with him in her apartment, she was too scared to get them scuffed in the street. He even bought her a new pair of sunglasses when he accidentally crushed hers during a particularly sudden sexual escapade in a naughty location. They were some high-end American brand, Miyako wasn't sure which one.

Andrew slipped off the bed to face her and kneeled before her. Miyako was confused and wondered if he was about to tear off her underwear. Where was her present? From his front pocket, he revealed a tiny box which he presented to Miyako. He opened it to reveal a golden ring with a white diamond.

"Oh it's so pretty! It looks like a star," Miyako said. She'd never received a ring from a soldier before. She was enchanted with the new gift. It was indeed expensive and fit into the twinkling star theme of many of Andrew's presents. Bracelets, necklaces, even the sunglasses he given her dazzled. She wondered how it would look if her nails were polished in blue instead of red.

"I'm glad you like it."

Miyako put on the ring and admired the sparkling gem on her finger. It seemed to have a life of its own, like bubbling champagne something Miyako only tried once before it went straight to her nose and caused her to sneeze on one of her dates. Connor slept with her anyway, despite the gunk.

"Oh thank you!" She fell on top of Andrew and held him tight as he laughed. She was already super horny from the gift. She was prepared to start blowing him right there on the bed.

"So your answer is yes?"

"Yes. Of course," Miyako answered. "Of course I want this! I thought you were coming today to break-up with me! I'm so relieved."

"I could never leave you," Andrew was stroking the back of her head now. "So you'll marry me?"

Miyako then realized the depth of the question. What he'd been silently asking through such an expensive gesture. How could she be so stupid? Years ago an American explained to her a ring was used to ask for marriage, hence why he'd never gifted her one. In fact, many of her clients told her their stories of failed and successful marriage proposals, all involving diamond rings. She quickly moved her head to face him and cocked a smile. The seriousness of his face scared her. She took a moment to let it sink in. How could she respond to such a question? She had to tell him now, right then and there. She needed to give him an answer. Otherwise, she was going to hurt him very badly. Hurting an American hero was the last thing she ever wanted to do. Before she could say no, revealing she hadn't understood his request until just then, Andrew spoke again.

"Great," he said.

Miyako was relieved he looked like himself again. She decided not to disappoint Andrew just yet. She would let him dream for the night, or however long she could let him. She wasn't sure when she was going to be able to tell him no. She only wanted to make her favorite clients happy.

She concentrated on making love to him. At least, she could truthfully please him that way. She blew him for as long as her lips could handle, until he flipped her over and made his way inside her. She let sex become an excuse to not have to say anything else for now. She used her body to say other things inside, things, which didn't complicate or ruin anything. Things which revealed her deep love for him, despite knowing she would have to say no. Avoid a request she couldn't fulfill.

While Andrew slept, Miyako looked to the ceiling as thoughts formed tide pools inside her mind. Why did she have to say no? Couldn't she just say yes to make him happy and thus make herself happy too? She knew the truth even if it was selfish and unrealistic.

She loved Andrew, but it wasn't the same way she loved other clients. But it went beyond that. He wasn't her dream soldier. How would she be able to ever tell him something like that? How would she ever be able to tell him he wasn't enough? After all, he'd done in the military? After how brave he'd been? After how kind he'd been to her despite everything he'd been through? After how well he pleased her in bed, his oral skills were still lacking. After offering her another life? He hadn't told her what he had in mind upon marrying her, but she knew laws were changing so Americans could bring their Japanese wives back to the U.S. To the magic land who given birth to all her favorite heroes.

She didn't have the courage to tell him even as he left the next morning. She just faked a smile when he told her how wonderful their lives would be together. How great a husband he'd be, how he'd live showing her off as his wife, and how much better her life would be in America. How could he not tell she was faking? But she didn't want to break his dream just yet. Was that the only reasons she hesitated to tell him the truth? She hid the ring inside a sock and closed it into her drawer.

***

Miyako realized after the next few days of mind-blowing sex with other clients, perhaps in comparison, Andrew's lovemaking skills were only adequate. And he asked her to settle for that for the rest of her life? She'd go mad.

With each man, she orgasmed more than usual. Everything was intensified. A man was putting all of his hopes on her, and here she was fucking her brains out with other men. The thought of it turned her on then got her off again and again.

When she'd finished, guilt set in. She had to tell Andrew the truth. If she cared for him, she needed to release him to find a good wife.

***

Roger asked Miyako to meet him among the Cherry Blossoms. The trees were still in bloom, proving not much time had passed. Yet so much happened in Miyako's life since the first flower bloomed for the season. The flowers were beginning to wilt and fall off the branches, but they were still beautiful. Sometimes it would rain pink upon her and she would dance in the cascade of petals.

Roger told her it was for a picnic and he volunteered to bring lunch. She'd been surprised by his sentiment. He told her on their last date that he was leaving in a month or so. Perhaps it was time for good-byes.

She was embarrassed to have cried in front of him after he told her. She kept telling him it was fine, she'd be okay, and she was happy he was going back to his wonderful country. She told him not to worry about her and she would miss him but she was happy for him. He refused to have sex with her that night and held her in bed instead. At first, she thought her tears took her sexiness away. Shinju told Miyako crying made all girls look ugly. But the way he held her told there was something he wasn't saying to her just yet.

Something he would say among the cherry blossoms, Miyako surmised.

Miyako often told Roger how much she loved the flowered trees. They were her favorite thing on Earth. She told him of the kinds of spirits which dwelled there. Kodama dwelled in the oldest of the trees, making them sacred, and kami swung from branch to branch, invisible to human eyes. She told him no matter how hard the seasons or how bad the war got, the flowers always came. They were a reminder that beauty, goodness, simplicity, love, joy, would always find a way. After the war, their beauty proved life, while short and delicate, was worth living. She loved the way he smiled when she would finish telling him about those flowers. It was a special smile he reserved for those flowers.

A smile he showed off as they walked among the trees. They both remarked on the beauty of the flowers but mostly observed them in silence and awe. Miyako was so happy he was able to appreciate this with her. Even after all he'd seen in the war, Japan held beauty and magic for him.

Roger told Miyako to find her favorite tree for their picnic. Miyako picked one of the smaller trees among the larger ones. She liked it despite its size. All of its flowers seemed vibrant and large compared to the other trees. They sat down to eat. Roger pulled salmon sandwiches, strawberries, and Rose wine from a basket. Pink a starring role in the ensemble of food. Miyako was delighted by the sentiment.

They ate and smiled at each other. Miyako was looking forward to kissing him.

"Oh! I almost forgot dessert!" Roger said as they finished their meal.

Miyako laughed. "I hope it's chocolate! I'm going to be sadder about you leaving if it isn't!"

"I guess you're going to be disappointed then."

Roger pulled out a blue box from the basket and went on one knee in front of Miyako. Her eyes widened. Was this really happening to her again?

It was.

He was proposing to her. He opened the box to reveal a beautiful silver ring with a pink diamond matching the petals surrounding it.

"I wanted to get you one as beautiful as your favorite flower, since you're my favorite flower," Roger said.

Miyako began to cry.

"I don't understand, you said you were leaving."

"I am, but after some thinking I realized you could come with me. And why not? You're the best part of this strange country."

Miyako laughed. She was tempted to tell him she'd been proposed to a few days before, but she dared not ruin the moment for either of them. She was going to turn down Andrew anyway.

"So what do you say?" he asked. "Will you marry me? Be my Sakuya to my Ninigi?"

He'd remembered the story of the God who chosen to marry the Goddess of the cherry blossoms instead of the Goddess of rocks. Hence why human life wasn't long like stone but short and beautiful like the pink flowers.

What would it mean for her if she said yes to Roger?

Before, Miyako thought about it, she nodded as she continued to cry. This was it. This was the most romantic proposal a girl could ever hope for. How could she say no? But, she feared giving up all she ever knew, the love of all the men, her country even though she abandoned its customs long ago, her freedom. What new world and life would she be walking into?

Roger was her favorite. He was the one she loved the most out of all the men. He didn't make her orgasm the most or give her the most expensive gifts. Out of all the men she'd been with, he was the one who worked to know her inside out.

They laid there and kissed among the cherry blossoms for a long time. Yet, it didn't feel as Miyako hoped it would. A voice raged in the back of her mind, screaming she was making a terrible mistake. The beauty of the moment among the cherry blossoms couldn't quiet these thoughts.

***

Dusk washed over the street as Miyako leaned in front of a closed toy store to smoke a cigarette.

"Will you marry me?"

The words sounded again in her ears. She paused then continued smoking her cigarette, eyeing the pink diamond as it shimmered with the last of the sunlight. She wondered if it could still sparkle in the moonlight. Just like stars.

Why did she feel so unhappy? Wasn't this what she should want? A choice between two men. Two men willing to get her out of the war-torn country and care for her in America. The one she picked would take her away to a beautiful place, and she was going to be happy forever. What girl was so lucky?

She was going to pick Roger who'd given her the prettier ring and who she loved the most.

What was holding her back?

Someone who might not even exist.

It was the man. That ideal American soldier. The one she still dreamed of. Her heart was telling her to wait for him. If she got married and went with one of the soldiers, he would never be able to find her.

Was she really crazy enough to wait on an imaginary man? That wasn't a good reason. She needed to be logical, she had to pick Roger.

With the blow of the wind, Miyako felt her power ignite. A chill moved through her throat and heart. It was so intense it almost knocked her to her knees.

"You always show up on cue."

Miyako looked up.

"Shinju!" she exclaimed.

"Long time no see."

Shinju took a long draw on her cigarette. The ashes on the end illuminated her face to reveal for a flickering moment the dark circles around Shinju's eyes. She looked old, weathered, beaten. Defeated. She was back on the decline again. The moment was gone before anyone would have noticed, except Miyako, as Shinju gracefully blew the image away through the smoke.

"Are you working?"

Shinju inhaled while looking down, "Not tonight. I have a headache."

"What are you doing here?"

"Smoking a cigarette. You blind?"

"It's just that I haven't seen you."

"I haven't seen you either."

"But I want to! I miss you!"

Shinju blew out smoke from the side of her mouth. "Liar."

"I'm not lying." Miyako was and wasn't.

"You've looked at me differently ever since you found out I worked in a brothel," Shinju exhaled. "Even though what we do is the same thing."

"I told you I didn't care about that Shinju! I just didn't understand why you hadn't told me."

"And why I didn't try to help those girls? Do you know why I really didn't?"

"You said it was because they were probably diseased."

"No. They hated me. They got me kicked out, so I had to start working on the streets." Shinju clicked her heels on the ground.

"Why did they do that?"

"I was stealing all their clients and money, apparently."

"Well, you are beautiful, you deserved them!"

"How naive you are, Miyako?"

Miyako saw the reflection of her wedding ring in Shinju's eyes.

"Who gave you the ring?" Shinju asked.

"Roger. But would you believe it? Andrew proposed to me too! Isn't it wonderful?"

"But I thought you liked all your boy toys. You're going to have to give them all up to just play with one. Or have you finally figured out you were a slut? So you're going to marry a guy, run away to America, and pretend it never happened?"

"Shinju…"

"I really hate how you say my name, you know that?"

"You could probably marry a guy too if you wanted. Find someone and come with me."

"You haven't exactly noticed I'm not marriage material have you?" She spit on the ground. "But neither are you."

The words flew into Miyako like blades. She thought of her lovers to calm herself.

"They love me. That's all that matters."

Shinju's responding cackle echoed down the street and into the night. She sounded like one of the creatures who belong to the darkness. She laughed until she slid down the side of the wall and landed on the ground. Her laughter slowly died as she sat there. Her predatory smile remained.

Miyako use to love how Shinju smiled and laughed. Now she hated it.

When Shinju finally finished, she rose to her feet and got close to Miyako. Miyako could smell her skin oozing with smoke and perfume.

"What makes you think they love you, Miyako?"

Miyako looked at her silently for several moments. Things to say swam through her mind. The way they looked at her, the gifts, the sex, the nice things they said to her, all of the intimacy, and moments they shared. Connections that went unspoken between her and her men. She knew none of this would satisfy Shinju.

"I just know." Miyako replied.

Shinju took a few steps back and smiled.

"How could so many men be in love with the same girl? How could that possibly be true? You really think the world revolves around you? That all of these men would leave their wives for some Japanese hooker? Even I believed you couldn't possibly be that stupid, but you proved me wrong."

Shinju lit another cigarette.

"There's different kinds of love, Shinju."

Shinju spit to the ground and turned her back on Miyako.

"The kind of love a man has one night for a hooker and the kind he has with his wife? What about his mommy?"

"If you want to put it that way Shinju, yes. But they need me. They need us. If their love from their other women was enough, they wouldn't come to us."

"It's all horniness from their stupid dicks. There's no heart there. They lay you to get what they want from you. They take from whatever woman they can get their fix. All men care about is sex. They only care about pleasing their needs. The Americans and Japanese are just the same that way. All men are."

Shinju's eyes were watery. Miyako never seen Shinju cry before. She wondered what dark secrets she hid. What she'd seen turning her bitter as the years wore on. Aging and killing her inside.

"They give back too. I've gotten so much from them. They've given me money and freedom. A life of pleasure beyond anything I could have known. They've taught me so much about the world."

"Like what? All of the places a guy can stick his dick?"

"That's the least of it."

"Then what? I'm listening." Shinju waited with her cigarette which she left to burn between her fingers.

Miyako didn't know if her explanation would be worth giving, but she felt no reason not to speak.

"They've given me a chance to heal."

"Pfft…what?"

"Just listen until I'm finished. Then you can make fun of me." Miyako was surprised at her own assertive tone toward Shinju. She continued, "The war tore the world apart. It ripped into each soldier and each civilian. It hurt all of us deeper than anything else ever has. It made our sorrows graver and gave us more things to cry about into the night. We stood in the doorway between life and death. Death becomes a faithful ally in life, for it held a certainty life never could. While we clung to life, we wished to surrender to death. When the war ended, and we survivors were given life without death, it made things seem even worse. There was no escape. No war to distract from the pain."

Miyako sighed. She gave Shinju an angry look to ensure she wouldn't interrupt as she took a moment to breathe.

"We were given the gift of life, denied to so many by the war. Wasting it would be an insult to the dead, but most of all to ourselves. Being able to live and love among these men, even along with you, has given me an understanding of how full life can be. I wouldn't have known that if it wasn't for the war. War taught me the value of life, of really living a full life. Even if it isn't one my family or country would be proud of. But it's a life I can be proud of."

She took a breath again. This time no look was needed to keep Shinju quiet.

"Besides the wonderful stories I've heard and the memories I now hold so dear, I've shared something so special with these men. Love. It's not the kind of love that's typical of a marriage. I don't know a lot about marriage, I am certain of that. But with these men, I've been able to share the joys of being alive this way. Sex makes the world so much more beautiful. As does pleasure and romance. Even the more serious times were painted more beautifully because we finally had what we needed. The good feelings, which come from truly living. Despite what happened between our wars and countries, we're able to share that together. It shows we're all connected somehow, through our connection in those moments."

"That's what you think you've gotten out of it? You're a loony."

"Haven't you gotten something out of it, too?"

"Money…but even that isn't worth it. It never was."

"Then why did you do it?"

Shinju knocked her cigarette to the ground and stomped it with her heel.

"It was the only thing I was ever good at," Shinju said as she kept her eyes to the ground. "Lying on my back and letting these stupid men have their way with me. Lying that I was enjoying it. Lying to myself, as have you. That or you really are stupid."

"I may have been naive when you brought me into this, but you and the Americans have made me otherwise. You gave me this life. I never realized you hated it so much."

"Most women in our position do. You seem to be the exception."

Shinju sighed and looked deep into Miyako's eyes.

"And the irony is, you're the one who gets the way out. You really never felt shame in any of this? You never saw this as a pitiful last resort? That I picked you because I knew you were just as bad off or worse off than me?"

"It was a choice I was willing to make. One I had to."

"And you're choosing marriage now? You can't be willing to love this life that much if you're willing to leave it."

Shinju looked at Miyako and grinned.

"You don't want to get married. You want to stay here right in Japan with your boy toys. You've tricked yourself into thinking this a good life. You wouldn't even know how to be a wife, would you? Do you even know how to cook and clean? How to make clothes?"

"My mother taught me, plus I had training in Gion in which I...."

Shinju interrupted her. "You don't look happy about it. You only seemed happy when you talked about this job. So why are you getting married, really?"

Miyako shrugged, "I guess it's what you're supposed to do. But truly, I don't know."

"A woman so willing to defend the lifestyle of a whore can't even convince me of benefits of marriage. What? Can't be satisfied with one man?"

Miyako slapped Shinju. Miyako hadn't realize what she'd done until she felt the sting in her lowered hand. Shinju smiled as if she'd enjoyed it. The look she gave was the same one Miyako seen on the first day she met her. Fox eyes. Eyes with the deeper mystery and knowing. She wondered what things Shinju knew that Miyako didn't. She suddenly felt less confident in her resolve.

"Follow me," said Shinju. "I want to show you something before you get married. Even though I don't think you're going to go through with it."

Miyako felt her intuitive powers go ablaze. Fire and ice raged inside her. She thought she'd exhale them at the same time, like a dragon, if she breathed too hard. Yet, she ignored these feelings, for the sake of honoring her mentor, and followed Shinju into the darkness.

***

Miyako lagged behind Shinju. She felt no desire to walk alongside her. Shinju was disappearing into the dark, and Miyako feared she'd vanish with her.

Shinju led Miyako into a thick forest. Blackness enveloped them. Miyako's heart quickened its pace. She'd forgotten to wear her blue lipstick. What spirits lingered here? She prayed to the kodama for assistance. Hoped at least one kami was on her side. For the first time in years, Miyako feared the night.

Miyako touched an old tree and tucked the sound of her prayer into the passing wind.

Shinju stopped, but kept her eyes ahead.

"Still hold the superstitions of our ancestors? That's not what you're going to find here. What I brought for you to see is under my feet."

Miyako shuffled closer to Shinju. She followed Shinju's eyes to the disturbed ground below.

"What's this?" Miyako asked.

"I'd stolen my gun from a soldier. He'd fallen asleep while drunk and I saw it hidden in the pocket of his jacket. I never wanted something so much in my whole life. I took it away from him as he'd taken my body from me over and over again. I left him in the night before he'd even knew what happened. I feared he'd find me, but I never saw him again. I know in my heart now that he'll never come after me." She continued. "I always kept the gun with me after that. I even slept with it next to my pillow when I was alone." She pulled it out to show Miyako. "It became my best friend."

Miyako could only see the shape of the gun in the darkness. She couldn't see or feel anything reminding her of friendship. Fear flowed through her veins, and her heartbeat could no longer keep up with her lungs. An old tree caught her fall, so she remained on her two feet.

"I finally had something to protect me. Something that would follow only my will. No matter how far I needed it to go."

Shinju pointed the gun to the earth.

"A man beat me and dragged me out here. He'd intended to rape me and kill me. I could hear it in his thoughts. His eyes told me the same thing. Before he could even take off his pants, I shot him. I told him how much I hated the Americans. How much I hated the Japanese. How much I hated men for what they do to women and the world. How their desire for power and their blind devotion following the urges of their dicks would destroy everything. Unless something else ended them first."

Shinju smiled.

"I told him that before he died. Before my best friend killed him and saved me from this evil man."

Shinju looked to the disturbed ground.

"While I couldn't punish them all. I managed to punish one. He will forever remain here, defeated by his own stupid masculinity. Dying under the tool of war, he'd tried to dominate by. He took himself to his own grave. His own worm food for other worms. A fitting end for any man."

Shinju turned the gun on Miyako.

"Take off your clothes."

Miyako kept her hands on the tree. This time she wouldn't follow such an order.

"Take off your clothes and play with your pussy. Just like you love to do for those disgusting men. If you're lucky, I'll kiss it before I kill you."

"What's the meaning of this Shinju?" Miyako kept her voice calm. It was too late to show fear or plead. She needed to keep cool now whether it led to escape or death.

"I want you dead! I hate you!"

"Why Shinju? What made you hate me?"

"Are you pleading for your life?"

"You're the one who gave me this life. It's within your right to take it away. I've lived more fully in these last few years than I could have otherwise."

"It's a shitty life!"

"That's how you see it, but my experience has been very different. I owe you everything, including my life."

"Falling back to old traditions this late? Trying to die honorably?"

"Tradition doesn't involve me asking you personal questions. And that's not how I want to go out. I want to know you, Shinju. I've always wanted to understand you. You hid so much for me. Let me see you before you kill me."

"You've seen my whole body. You fucked me against my will."

"If you want to kill me for that reason, I'll accept death. But your body doesn't tell me who you are. You've had my body. I've told you about myself. Let you in as far as I could before you shut out my words. Now let me see you. You do that and I'll go quietly. I won't haunt you as a hungry spirit. But you must do this first."

"You really want to know?"

"Yes."

"Fine, Shinju huffed and lowered the gun. She took a few minutes to collect her thoughts. After a few deep breaths, she spoke. "As a child I lived on a farm with my family. All boys. A father, some brothers, and no mother. I dreamed of becoming a Geisha. To be among beautiful women. But it wasn't just for the company. I loved women."

Shinju paused. Her face contorted for a moment and then smoothed again. "Since I was a little girl, I'd masturbate to fantasies of touching another woman as I saw my father do. He fucked our neighbor one night, even though she was married. She never came back to our home, but I remembered how beautiful her body was and how ugly my father was. I'd get so horny when I'd see her around town. I dreamed of kidnapping her, ripping off her clothes, and taking her whole. Making love to her better than my father ever could. But she left when her husband died. I never saw her again."

Shinju eyes glossed over. She was no longer in the woods with Miyako. She'd gone back in time through her memories.

"I knew even then my feelings weren't natural. Men were supposed to want women. Women were only supposed to want men. But men were unworthy of beautiful women. It drove me mad."

Shinju spit at the dirt below. She continued.

"When I was a teenager, Mineko was blooming into a beautiful woman. I loved her dearly. She was beautiful. Like a peach. Her breasts were tender like a fruit. She always smelled like a peach too. She reminded me of a fox when she smiled. I went out of my way to befriend her. At first, I told myself I just wanted to be near her. I would keep my desire for women a secret, from her especially. When I was alone, I'd masturbate and imagine how things would have gone if I'd followed my desires. If I'd kissed her, if I'd took off her clothes, if I'd fucked her. But soon, fantasy wasn't enough for me."

Shinju grinned in the darkness.

"One day I managed to make love to her. I told her it was practice for our future husbands. I told her all girls did this secretly in preparation for marriage. She bought the story. She let me feel her every part. I kissed her pussy so many times she actually climaxed for me. She tasted like peaches there too. She was perfect. She was mine. At least for the time I made love to her, she belonged to me. I controlled her. Touching her anyway I saw fit. Making her orgasm to my will. Climaxing as I used her."

Miyako sneezed and peed on the roots of the tree. Shinju was still looking at the ground, seemingly unaware of the interruption.

"It was the only time things felt somewhat right to me. When we would be naked together and I was free to touch her how I wanted. Watching her move and make noise based on what I did to her. Reaching into her most sensitive parts and touching what was forbidden to me as a woman myself. When she would touch me back, it was as if I was being given a divine gift. She never asked me when we were going to be done practicing, so I continued. There were times I was able to take her several times daily."

Miyako's legs itched, but she remained still. In the distance, a fox crossed her line of vision. It stopped to watch them. It was then Miyako knew she was going to live.

"I wanted to keep her forever. I was going to convince her to go to a Geisha house with me so we could be together. So, I'd never have to see her with another man. I couldn't imagine her soft insides, so supple and perfect, succumbing to a penis. Perhaps I could convince her to keep practicing with me. Or perhaps she enjoyed fucking me too and would be fine with me finally presenting it as it was. Then we could be lovers secretly for the rest of our lives. We hadn't been discovered. Perhaps we never would be. We had a chance at being happy."

Shinju sighed. The fox gaze pierced the darkness. Its eyes shined like stars in the sky.

"But a brother of hers caught us before we could make it to Gion. Mineko got off easy, I was grateful for that. They sent her to Gion without me to become a Geisha. At least, I didn't have to worry about a man ruining her now. I was considered trouble in my town so they assumed I'd forced her into it. They were right."

Shinju looked down at the ground again. The fox vanished into the forest.

"My father hated me then. Told me it was unnatural for women to do what I'd done. That I was some kind of demon. He beat me for days. When I'd thought I would die, I was exiled from my home. I became a prostitute to survive. I couldn't kill myself even though I knew I was a monster. When I was caught making love to another woman, I lost my job. I was forced to work the streets on my own. Find another way to survive."

Shinju looked into Miyako's eyes. "I thought I could destroy that part of me. Repent for my sins of loving women, by letting men have me. I don't even remember who was the first. I let men inside of me because there was nothing there for them to ruin. I was never a real woman inside since I couldn't love men. I thought fucking enough men would kill that part of me. Numb me of my own desires. But after all the dicks which made their way in and out of me, my love of women has remained."

Shinju's eyes began to glisten like diamonds. "I thought of you every time I fucked another man."

Shinju dropped the gun and began to cry. "I'm sorry. I never wanted to hurt you. It's just you're the only reminder of this thing inside me. This unnatural desire for the same sex."

"Shinju…"

"Do you enjoy women?" Shinju interrupted before Miyako could say more.

"Not in the same way as you."

"You enjoy men more. I can tell. It's unnatural for two women to be together. You've only enjoyed being with me because you didn't know better. Because you trusted me. Yet, I still feel every man who fucked you ruined you somehow. See how sick I am? I'm the one who brought you into this wretched life. I gave you to men who ruined you with their dicks. I can't believe you've enjoyed it. These men use you until they go home to their real women. You're just a warm pretty body to get them through their boredom and loneliness. Too bad there are no prostitutes for women. That would have been a good living for me."

Shinju bent down to pick up the gun on the ground.

Miyako felt a jolt come from the tree she'd been clutching and ran. She wasn't going to take a chance even though her intuition told her Shinju was no longer a threat to her. She zigzagged between the trees to make it harder for Shinju to land a shot on her, something the American soldiers said they had been trained to do. A few told her doing this saved their lives. Yet she was sure Shinju wouldn't fire the gun. She never heard a shot. All she heard was the cry of foxes running alongside her and her body swishing through the forest.

Miyako didn't stop running until she'd escaped the woods. By then, her heartbeat had become painful. Her breathing hurt as well. Miyako kept looking behind her. Shinju didn't emerged from the woods.

Miyako made it back to her apartment and locked her door then jumped into bed. Miyako hid under the covers, holding as still as she could as she clutched a teddy bear, fearing Shinju would knock at any moment. No knocking came. After hours went by, she finally fell asleep.

When Miyako awoke, she noticed her ring's sparkle was dulled and the promise it represented. She took it off and hid it inside the same sock she'd hidden Andrew's ring. She looked at the lump the rings formed in the cloth. She took them out and stared at them in her hand. Neither of them felt right anymore. Back into the sock and drawer they went. Miyako didn't want anyone else to know she was engaged.

***

Weeks went by without incident. Yet, Miyako was haunted by nightmares. She didn't remember most of them, but she'd woken up as she dreamed of bombs and gunfire. Once she saw Shinju being dragged by bloody hands into her own grave. Sex provided an easy means to avoid sleep. She felt safer resting in bed with her lovers. Only then would she allow her eyes to close.

But her lovers couldn't protect her from the flood of bad dreams cursing her sleep. They too were helpless to their own nightmares of war.

Sleep bound them from rescuing each other until the horror finished its course only to repeat itself too soon.

***

Harry was almost the perfect lover. His voice was slightly off as well as his gift giving skills. But his knowledge of the world and his skills in the bedroom far surpassed many of her other clients. He also had a penis that fit her like a glove. Filling her perfectly as it massaged her insides.

She'd failed to mention her engagement to him. For tonight, she wanted things to be the same. Every night following her engagement was met with the same excuse.

He wasn't the first client she'd seen since her proposal from Roger, and she knew he wouldn't be the last. She would have to see Andrew one more time to give him his ring back. Roger wouldn't be available for a while longer, and he hadn't been ready to make the marriage arrangements. Miyako figured it wouldn't be any harm to continue seeing her other clients in the meantime. After all, she was still a single woman.

After a romantic dinner over burgers, fries, cokes, and milkshakes, Harry led Miyako back to their favorite hotel. They even tried to get the same room each time since Harry loved entertaining Miyako's love of the number eight.

Pop.

Harry pulled out a gun and ordered Miyako to get behind him. His demeanor changed instantly as he prepared for combat. His face went blank. His eyes showed preparation for survival and killing. He was back in the war. This frightened her.

Down the street in front of a bar, Miyako saw Shinju standing across from a soldier who looked to be about eighteen. To his side lay a body of a young soldier, close to the same age.

The boy was trembling and his groin was wet. Shinju was screaming at him about how much she hated all men. How they were all scum. How the Americans acted like they were fixing Japan while they were ruining it further. How the Japanese and American men ruined her life. How they were ruining the women of Japan. The boy was frozen in fright. Shinju pulled out her gun and pointed it at him. Before Miyako had a chance to scream, Shinju was tackled by three other GIs who then held her to the ground. Harry was already pulling Miyako away from the sight. She could barely hear what he was saying to her, all she heard was another gunshot. Then another. And another.

Miyako slipped from Harry's grasp as she ran toward Shinju. Harry cursed and ran after her. Then she saw a body on the ground. Three tiny holes oozed with blood. All three shots had been at Shinju. One to the head and two below in areas Miyako couldn't bear to look. She was already still in death. How could something so terrible happen so fast? This was a scene from one of her nightmares. Miyako knew despite the surreality of it all, despite her disbelief, her only friend in the world was dead.

Shinju, flawlessly beautiful in life, made an ugly corpse. Her rouge and eyeliner smeared across her taut face. Black racooned her eyes. Shinju was crying before she died. Her clothes were dirty and torn. Her eyes bulged in anger and shock upon being shot by a man. A gun hadn't been her best friend after all, but a blind and silent witness as its doppelganger killed her. Perhaps Shinju wanted to be destroyed. Murdered by her own hatred of men.

Miyako reached down to touch her friend. She still felt life in the wisp of her hair, but she felt that quickly fading. Those parts of her body couldn't outlive the rest of her for long. From behind, Miyako felt the heat of a man coming from behind her. Before she could react, he fell over, like a tree in a forest. Harry had punched him.

"Let this one go. She's with me."

Harry pulled himself behind Miyako and pulled her away. She felt like a child.

"It's not safe here," he said. "There's nothing you can do now."

Miyako managed to grab Shinju's sunglasses before Harry dragged her away from Shinju. The men crept toward Shinju like a vulture as Miyako drew further and further away. She heard their drunken shouts and laughs growing softer as her distance from the scene widened.

She heard more gunfire. She did her best not to imagine what was happening behind her. She tucked the glasses down her dress so they would touch her heart.

Miyako cried all the way to the hotel room. Silently so Harry wouldn't notice. His concern for her only occasionally peeked through his anger. Miyako felt deep shame. She'd forced him to fight another battle he needed no part in. Just as the Japanese needlessly extended the war.

"Why'd you do that? You could have gotten us both killed! Those men were drunk, and that woman shot one of their own! There was nothing you could have done for her."

Miyako remained quiet, and he didn't ask her any more questions as they marched on. His emotions remained wild.

Once they got to the hotel room Harry calmed himself. Once again, he put his life of combat in the past. He apologized for his reaction and kissed Miyako for a long time on her neck and mouth. She didn't move back. He took some of her clothes off before he noticed she was crying.

"What's wrong?"

Miyako couldn't speak and looked to the bed, doing her best to try to pull the rest of her clothes off. He held her hands to stop her and looked into her eyes.

"Did you know her?"

After a long pause, Miyako nodded.

"I'm sorry, I didn't know."

"Do you know what will happen to her now?" Miyako said.

"I wish I could tell you."

"Are the police going to get involved? Are they going to get in trouble for hurting her?"

"I'm sure they will." But Miyako saw the truth in his eyes.

"No, they won't."

Harry sighed.

"All right. They might get in some trouble from their officers, but it's unlikely Japan is going to do anything. Japan doesn't care for girls like that."

"Girls like me." Miyako looked at him.

"You're not the same, Miyako."

"Yes, I am."

"Miyako."

"My clients just like me a lot better. She didn't serve as well. That's the only difference. I stop pleasing my clients, and I'll end up just like her."

"She was at a notoriously dangerous bar, Miyako."

"She wanted to die."

Harry was quiet for a few moments before breaking the silence.

"If that's the case, there was nothing you could have done. When someone wants to die, no one can stop them. I've learned that the hard way."

Just like Drew.

They sat on the bed quietly. Miyako was grateful for the silence they shared. She watched Harry's face. His eyes traveled back in time. For the one friend she'd lost, Harry lost so many more in the war. How many died before his very eyes? She'd let him keep that a secret. Some things a man couldn't bear to tell a woman.

How many Americans ended their own lives after surviving the war because they remained ensnared in its horrors? How many Japanese soldiers suffered the same way? How many were kept silent by duty or culture and faced the war's continuation within themselves. Alone. How many succumbed to the terrors that haunted them?

Her American heroes were still human. As were the Japanese. Ordinary men enduring extraordinary circumstances. Miyako expected war to turn worthy men into gods. But it was a battle just to keep their humanity intact.

"We can't have sex tonight."

"Understandable. I'll still pay you."

"I'm not worried about that. But will you do something for me?"

"What?"

Miyako pulled out the sunglasses from between her breast.

"This is all I have left of my friend. I don't think they're going to give her a proper burial. In fact, I'm sure they're not. I don't want to imagine what's going to happen to her body. I know I'm not going to be able to find it.

She's hurt other men, but there's good to her too. I want to honor her life."

Miyako continued to stare at the sunglasses.

"I'm not going to be able to bury this in the cemetery during daylight. If I go tonight, I might end up getting caught by the police. Can you come with me right now?

Harry nodded.

***

All the way to the cemetery, Harry held Miyako's hand. She wanted him and didn't want him at the same time. It was a slow walk to reach the dead. Miyako dragged her feet into the ground. It was as if they were both carrying Shinju's body, a heavy weight lingered over them. All the while, Miyako felt watched. *A Kitsune or Shinju's ghost already wandering across the lonely Earth*, Miyako thought.

They arrived at the cemetery. Miyako walked there occasionally to clear her thoughts. To remind herself, there was peace in death. To remember and honor those who died in the war even though most of their bodies were interred far way. To remind herself to appreciate the life she had left. It was a beautiful place to be compelled to do so.

She thought she saw a ghost in the cemetery the first time she walked by. But upon entering, nothing was there. She'd been visiting since, hoping to catch a glimpse of the other side while finding peace in the silence death offered.

Miyako scanned the grounds for the sunglasses final resting place, already knowing which patch of dirt to go to, but needing to recognize it in the dark. Once she located the spot, she approached it quickly, letting go of Harry's hand. The smell that mysteriously lingered was the giveaway she'd found it. It was a spot which always emitted the scent of perfume, Miyako wasn't sure why. But it was perfect for Shinju. Perhaps this grave had been calling to her all this time. Miyako shook off memories of her nightmares so she could continue her task.

She knelt in the earth as if in a prayer to allow her friend into the afterlife. Despite the lack of a body or ash, she hoped the offering of sunglasses would somehow be enough to repent for Shinju's sins and let her find peace in death.

Miyako dug a small hole near a tree that twisted its way to the sky. When she was far away enough, and when it was almost dark, she often saw a fox peering at her from behind this tree. Miyako often wondered if it was a real fox, a Kitsune, or ghost. There was no fox tonight. Miyako still felt eyes on her that weren't Harry's. She carefully placed the glasses in the hole and returned the displaced earth to its home. Something felt filled inside of Miyako as well. Harry put an arm around Miyako's waist. They both stood above the miniature grave, silently.

"What do Americans do with their dead?" Miyako asked.

Harry hesitated for a moment.

"You mean at the wake? The whole process or just the burial?"

"Just the burial. A client of mine told me what happens at wakes. He was too scared to go to the funeral, so I don't know what they're like."

"They usually bury people with their families and friends around. A priest reads some holy words above them while the living watches. Then they're put in the ground."

Harry was quiet before asking, "What do the Japanese do?"

"I don't remember. That was all another lifetime."

"I could get an ordained friend of mine to swing by in the morning and say a prayer for your friend."

"I see. Well there's no priest here, so I'll have to make do with what we have right now. I'm afraid if we wait too long it will be too late for her spirit."

"I'll still ask my friend to say some words in the morning. But yes, some kind words would be soothing to the dead now."

Miyako took a breath. She could have interpreted Harry's words as just validation to her beliefs, not because he believed but more that he felt the need to soothe her. But deep down she knew he too believed in the afterlife. It comforted her.

Miyako found most of her soldiers sensed something beyond the world of human eyes. Perhaps their close encounters with death broke the fabric between here and there. Death can't be ignored when constantly surrounded by it. In the midst of war, there's no escape from death.

Veterans told Miyako about seeing ghosts on the battlefields, wandering aimlessly, or still fighting. A few received messages from dead comrades in their dreams. One over the radio while men from his platoon stood in earshot and awe.

Soldiers told her ghost stories off of the battlefield as well. In old houses and bedrooms. At funeral homes and parks. Encounters they discounted until war made them realize they hadn't imagined any of it after all. Some even witnessed miracles in the midst of war. Powerful forces who intervened whether seen or unseen, Angels, they called them. Even when it was clear an ancestor came to their aid.

American spirits seemed to always look like people. The Japanese saw spirits, which looked human, but there were others which didn't appear human at all. The Americans didn't seem to see the other kinds of spirits the Japanese did. She wasn't sure why this was. Perhaps only certain cultures were open to seeing certain spirits, or the spirits changed based on who viewed them.

Perhaps even the ones who said they didn't believe still did deep inside, remaining afraid or jaded by the complexity of the world. Perhaps this was something binding all people, this knowledge of the spirit world. Miyako liked thinking that.

With Harry by her side, Miyako had the strength to say said good-bye.

"You opened my joy and pain. May you find peace."

Miyako turned to Harry, "Thank you Harry." She kissed him on the cheek, sweetly, as if tasting a fruit.

The pair turned and walked back to the hotel. On the way, Miyako pondered if Shinju would go to a peaceful afterlife or reincarnate. Perhaps she would become a fox or even a Kitsune. Shinju could be sexy even in her afterlife, but she could be happier on her new path. She could turn into a fox whenever she needed a break from people and turn back into human form when she longed for contact. She could enchant women instead of men and they would be helpless in their attempts to resist her. Once Shinju would look at a girl in the eyes, they would be under her spell. Shinju would be able to have whomever she wanted and she would be protected as a Kitsune. The thought of it made Miyako smile.

Despite, Miyako's insistence of being able to perform, Harry refused to have sex with her that night. Miyako was grateful, she wouldn't have had her heart in it anyway. She wanted to show her appreciation to him and didn't otherwise know how. She hoped her words were enough.

For a few hours, Miyako thought she was okay. She told herself she wouldn't have to cry anymore. She would be happy because Shinju would be okay, wherever she went and whatever she became. So would she. But despite this, Miyako felt the sadness creep up in her again. Some of it from fear and doubt, but most of it came from feeling the hollowness Shinju left behind. It was physically painful and Miyako was scared it would eat her alive. Harry held her all night as she cried over Shinju.

Had she'd worn her blue lipstick? She didn't remember. Harry may have been the only reason she was alive.

She left the next morning before he woke up. Miyako didn't want to burden him anymore. He'd done enough.

***

Miyako needed to be alone with her thoughts. She was feeling great sadness all over again, just like the night before. How often would this cycle repeat itself? Was mourning so cyclical? The Japanese made it seem straightforward, but based on what the Americans told her about their loss, she knew her bouts of mourning were the reality. She didn't understand why her family made her think dealing with death was so simple. Why despite her reeducation from the Americans she continued to return to what she was taught in childhood. She hoped at least she was smart enough to figure out the truth in all things. At this moment, she wanted to know how to deal with the permanent loss of Shinju.

Shinju was the only constant in her new life. She was the rock for the life Miyako had now. The same life Shinju hated. The same life that had killed her. It was true that Miyako still had Roger for almost as long, he somehow didn't serve the same purpose. He hadn't been her rock.

Miyako felt guilt rising within. Wasn't there anything more she could have done? But, Miyako knew Shinju never listened to anything she advised. Whether it was a change in lipstick or man. Certainly, Shinju wouldn't have taken any of Miyako's words seriously, even if she knew they'd prevent her own demise. Miyako had to stop returning to those thoughts, stop trying to convince herself she had any kind of control over Shinju's life. Miyako gave Shinju some control of hers for a time, but Shinju never let Miyako influence her. For better or worse, Shinju only listened to Shinju.

Would Shinju have killed her as she killed others? Even though Shinju spared Miyako's life that night, she could have found resolve to finish what she started another night.

Miyako shook her head. No, she told herself. Shinju changed her mind because deep down she loved her. That had to have been the reason right? At least at that moment. Love saved Miyako once again as it had many times before. But it was possible Shinju could have changed her mind again. And again. And again. But in between her conflict, Miyako could still have been dead.

What happened to her friend? Miyako was saddened when she realized she would never really know more than what she already did. She could spin it all in her head over and over again. Learned of Shinju's love of women sooner and forced her to talk about it. Accept it and find a lover who was the same. Prove Shinju could find a new life to take on as Miyako had through her. But each scenario Miyako conjured up in an attempted rescue coming all too late brought her to the same conclusion. Miyako couldn't save Shinju. Neither could the Americans. Many brought her more sorrow instead.

Still, she wished there had been another way.

Miyako wondered if her dream soldier would have been able to stop it. Sure, he may have saved Shinju at that moment, but people bound on self-destruction would destroy themselves when they got the chance. Harry made that clear.

Even her dream love couldn't stop someone's will to live or die. Miyako struggled as she continued to cycle her thoughts on Shinju over and over again until the day ended, or she surrendered to her exhaustion.

***

Miyako dreamed of encountering the men who shot Shinju. She chased them as a man would chase a woman. She had scared them, she saw it in their eyes. She demanded they expose their cocks or she would kill them with her fox powers. When they did, she laughed. They were so small. She called them bird food. She mocked them for exposing themselves and proceeded to eat their manhood.

She awoke shaking for a few moments before falling back asleep.

This time, she dreamed of flying among the stars, leaving her world far behind. The farther away she went the bigger she became. She was being filled with stars and sky, light and dark. Until she became the night itself.

Miyako woke up that morning, realizing the beautiful woman from the train station didn't exist in the first place. Shinju hid her true self under her sexy, wild, and confident facade. Miyako became someone from something that had never existed before. She was the real woman of the night. She smiled at that. She created that world, that image, that life. Shinju gave her a false dream, but Miyako weaved a beautiful existence from it. She made it real. She didn't owe anything to Shinju after all. Miyako did it all herself.

She could still create her life going forward. Take control of what was happening. She needed to.

She would start with Andrew.

***

Miyako lay on the hotel bed breezing through a Sears' catalogue. Andrew was letting her pick wedding gifts for herself. Perhaps she could get more treasures from him before she told him the truth. His gifts made her feel like the starry sky. Guilt over her gluttony was building to the point of breaking, but at that moment, she couldn't stop herself.

Miyako almost forgotten to put Andrew's engagement ring back on before she went to meet him, returning home to retrieve it after walking halfway to the hotel.

At first, she put on Roger's ring instead. Miyako loved it still despite her doubts. His ring spoke of the love story of the cherry blossoms. Andrew's ring sparkled like a star, appropriate for her line of work. But Roger's spoke of new hope, of a romantic life through an old story.

She resolved to take no more gifts from Andrew. It simply wasn't fair.

Andrew interrupted her line of thought as he called from the bathroom.

"I apologize. I've forgotten to shave, my dear. Let me take care of that now."

"Don't forget to trim near your penis!"

"I thought you liked my big dick!"

"I do! I mean your hair there, silly man!"

"Men don't need to trim there!"

"Yes, they do! It gets so itching otherwise! Itch for my poor gentle insides. I'm sure it does for you too if you keep it long like a wild beast."

"Ha. I know. I know. That's what I meant by trim. But I'm going to take care of this beard at the same time too. Hard to kiss a beautiful girl like yourself being all scruffy like this."

He closed the door of the bathroom. Miyako took refuge in the temporary boundary between them.

Miyako looked up at the mirror over the dresser across from the bed. Looking into her reflection, she imagined how a new red hat from the magazine would frame her face. Even though she knew, she wasn't going to ask Andrew for anything.

"Not exotic enough," she said quietly. "How do I look in red?" She shouted toward the closed door.

The only reply Miyako received was from the running water in the bathroom sink.

Miyako was shocked when she realized her first thought was about her clients. Not Andrew, not her actual future husband, and most importantly, not herself. Before she could ponder what any of this meant she noticed a shimmer at the edge of her vision. Both her eyes darted when she caught the sight of a beautiful white comb laying on dresser as if offering itself to her.

Miyako's eyes widened at the sight of it and she delicately closed the catalogue. She approached the comb as if it were a butterfly that would fly away in fear if she moved too quickly. When she was only a few inches away, she remained hesitant to touch the comb. She didn't know what to think. She'd never told Andrew the story.

Did he somehow know the story of her comb? Or was it some kind of coincidence? Perhaps fate brought it to her. This comb was the twin to the one she owned as a child. The flowers and pearls were the same. The same ebony that glowed like the moon. She'd forgotten about the comb until now. Fate simply used Andrew to remind her.

**

Since her family didn't have much money, she shared everything with her sister. There was nothing she could call her own. She resented her family for this, especially her sister. She hated how her sister got all of their things dirty despite how neat Miyako tried to be. A doll Miyako used in place of a friend became undesirable after her sister dove it into the mud. A nice dress she was given was ripped by her sister's little hands. A wooden toy cracked in a fight between the two of them, which Miyako was blamed and punished for, even though she'd simply been trying to protect her treasure.

Sometimes while Miyako roamed the market after buying vegetables and rice for her family, she'd check to see if her favorite comb was still in stock at the store. It always was. She'd eyed it, feeling a deep hunger and ache in every part of her body. She promised herself one day it would be hers. She never told her family or anyone about the comb. It was her secret, a treasure she coveted for herself.

One day she found a coin in the street. Instead of giving the money to her father, she went into the store and purchased the beautiful comb. She cried after she bought it. She walked to the local shrine, to ensure she could be alone. When she got there, she stared at the comb through her teary vision. She shook so hard she thought she'd collapse. She couldn't believe it was finally hers. She stayed there for hours, happy to finally have something truly hers.

She told no one anything about her comb. She hid it under her sleeping mat. This was partly out of shame but mostly to protect it from her sister. There she kept it for many months and no one discovered her purchase. Miyako used the comb in secret. She would wake herself up at night just to brush her hair in the moonlight. She desperately wanted to be beautiful. She longed to be hungered after as she hungered for more from the world. Dreaming of another life, she would gaze at the comb's jeweled radiance in the moonlight. Her mother commented her hair looked nicer once, but didn't dwell on it for long and never brought it up again. Her sister said nothing and only eyed Miyako's hair. For now, her secret was safe among the moon and stars.

Sometimes, Miyako would dream the God Susano transformed her into this comb in order to steal her away, undetected by her family. Once he got her far from home, he would return her to human form and make her his bride. From that moment on, her life would be perfect. It was always a happy dream. Yet, Miyako believed it could become real.

But one night, Susano failed to save her. That night she dreamed her family threw her into a pit with an eight-headed snake. Susano tried to rescue her by turning Miyako into a comb and tucking her in his long hair. While he fought the snake, she'd slip out and landed at his feet. Since she was a comb, she couldn't cry out to him. In the midst of the battle, he smashed the comb with his foot. She felt herself shatter into pieces, a pain exploded through her. She was dead, all her dreams were gone. She woke up in a cold sweat and cried out.

After her eyes adjusted back into the real world, she saw her sister not only found the comb but broken it trying to force it through a knot in her hair. It was snapped in two and stuck in her sister's tangles. Miyako leaped on top of her. She pinned her sister so she couldn't escape from her screams and fury.

"Why, why must you ruin everything that is mine? Why won't this family let me have anything to myself? Why are you so greedy, needing everything that is mine? I hate you! I hate you! I wish you'd die! I wish you hadn't been born. I hate this family that only cares about you. I want to destroy you. I want all of you destroyed."

Her sister cried. Miyako couldn't recall her sister ever crying like this before, but at that moment, she didn't care. Her tears made Miyako hit her, and when she cried harder, she hit her sister with more force. She was fueled by the little girl's distress. Miyako's scowl turned into a smile, happy to have some power in turning her sister into a victim. All her years of pent-up anger finally found release. It felt good. She laughed and hit her hard as she could with each blow. By the time her parents pulled her away, the damage was done. She was glad about that. Miyako saw in the midst of her rage she made her sister's nose and cheeks bleed. She was black and purple elsewhere. Revenge gave her a sense of calm head and she was ready to face any punishments to come.

Her parents didn't beat her in retribution as Miyako expected. They said nothing to her. They spoke gently to her sister and healed her face. Over the next few weeks, her sister was given the best of the meat and vegetables. Allowed extra time to rest and sleep. They spoke to her tenderly as her body mended itself and rewarded her progress with occasional toys and sweets.

Miyako waited for a punishment that never came. But they barely spoke to her after that.

She was a ghost in her own home, to her own family.

As time went on, they all became ghosts to her too.

While she later felt guilty for hurting her sister, she never apologized to her. She didn't speak to her after that. Her sister kept her head lowered when she was in her presence. Her sister never apologized either, which caused newfound anger in Miyako. But she'd grown to understand her family would never serve her and the sooner she could accept this, the better off she'd be. Miyako was more distressed over losing the comb and mourned its loss than anything else.

A few years after, she would still think of that beautiful comb and how she lost it. She felt the pain of that more deeply than the war, the famine that came with it, the lost lives of her brothers and father, and the pain she felt when she finally abandoned her family for good.

Then she'd been swept up into her new life. She hadn't thought about that comb for a long time.

Until now.

But how could she ever truly forget such pain. Her comb represented everything she ever wanted. Broken, it made her face her shattered hopes.

***

Miyako started brushing her hair as she gazed into the mirror. Tears flowed. A storm was emerging which had brewed within her for so many years. Maybe, Miyako was somehow directing her tears there on purpose.

Andrew opened the door and emerged with a bottle of white wine. She laughed a little to herself. He loved to hide surprises in the bathroom, as if she would never look there, and the sudden reveal would remain as mystical as some old magic trick. That was something she loved about him. His corny sense of romance. Realizing she couldn't marry him despite his good parts made her heart ache.

His smile faded, as if he heard her thoughts. But Miyako soon realized it was because he saw she was crying. He gently put the bottle of wine in front of the mirror and sat down next to Miyako.

"What's wrong?"

"It's so beautiful."

That was all Miyako could say.

"Then why is my gift making you cry?"

She didn't dare answer that question. Not to him. Perhaps there was another she could tell, but it wasn't him. She hated she was crying about this in front of him. He held her instead. It took her several minutes until she was able to hug him back. They hugged for a while and he stroked her back. He never held her this long before. Miyako found it sweet, but at the same time, she didn't want any of it from him. She desperately wished she was in the arms of another instead. Not even wanting that man to be Roger. She didn't want anything from him either now.

But right now, Miyako was with Andrew. She knew she couldn't accept such a gift knowing she couldn't stay and marry him. She was going to be honest with him. Right now.

"I can't marry you."

His silence shattered within moments.

"Why not?"

"Honestly, I don't think you love me. I've seen how you've looked at photos of that girl. Sometimes during sex and when you sleep at night, I hear you call her name."

He stared back blankly.

"You mean, Lily? She was a high school fling. But that's over now. She's married. I know she was pregnant when I left.

"It's okay, love is something hard to let go of. But that doesn't mean you should settle. You need to find a greater lover. Love which goes beyond the love you lost. Even if you feel like you can't find that, I won't be the replacement you need. Eventually, you'll resent me for not being that girl. After you offered a gift like this, I can't lie. I've actually said I was going to marry someone else."

Andrew was silent for a few moments. Hurt clearly written into the lines of his face. But it was soon erased by growing anger.

"When were you going to tell me?" His tone did very little to hide his emotions.

"You seemed so happy. I kept waiting, but you seemed so happy talking about it. You never even noticed I hadn't said yes. How was I to know you were going to notice a no?"

Miyako felt nervous but relief was flooding into her at the same time. She felt the reward of doing what was right. A cleared head and heart.

"So what were you going to do? Leave me at the altar? Marry us both! Who is this guy?"

"One of my clients."

"Clients? What do you mean?"

"One of the men I professionally love." Miyako looked into his eyes deeply.

"You're a prostitute?"

"I thought you were aware my job is to love whoever I'm with that night. You've paid me to love you.

Most of the men I see do. But I wouldn't call myself a prostitute."

"But that's what you are. A girl who fucking sleeps around with other people. I can't believe this. I gave you money because I felt sorry for you." His voice was increasing in speed and volume.

"Men sleep around too."

"What do you mean? Male prostitutes don't exist. Men don't fuck for money." Andrew overturned the dresser in the room as he emphasized the last word.

"Everyone gets something out of sex. And yes, men like to sleep around too. I've seen it for myself. I'm sure there are men who do it for money as well."

"I doubt that," he said darkly. "How can you live with yourself going off with all these men? And to think I was stupid enough to consider making you my wife?"

Miyako felt the cold overtake her. She no longer cared what he felt about her, but she was feeling rage building within her. Rage at how others were somehow unable to see the good in all she did. She used to believe such negative thoughts only came from the Japanese. The government embarrassed of her existence since she was a reminder of Japan's defeat. Feminists who looked to destroy her livelihood, believing she was a disgrace to all women. Police who worked to clean the streets of women of her kind. She did her best to ignore them all. Yet, they were a threat, and their power was growing. Soon it was going to be hard to make a living on romance in Japan.

Yet, the opinions of the Americans is what mattered to her. But even their opinion of her often fell short of what she desired. Andrew wasn't the only American to feel this way. He was just the first she cared for to say something to her. Other men she rejected called her out on her occupation, but she'd been too busy focused on her new clients to care. How many of her lovers judged her in secret and never said a word?

Words flowed out of Miyako's lips, like water from the mouth of a stream.

"You'd be surprised. I've seen enough now to not leave anything as an impossibility. Especially with how good sex feels, and how easily it brings money. When things got bad after the war, sex gave me an opportunity to transform. I became a lover. It changed me into someone who received and gave pleasure for the first time. I finally felt like I was doing something with my life. Something that would have lasting meaning, even in such transient acts as lovemaking. Giving beauty after the pains of the war. Showing life continues after death, even death caused by war."

Andrew's stillness scared Miyako. She continued.

"Sex is something everyone needs, I have yet to find a person who didn't need it. It's a rarity if that's the case for anyone. A lot of people either go around starving for it, or feeling like they need to hide the fact they've been getting their fill. But there are men who get bragging rights, a chance to try out things they would never dare dream on their beloved wives. Men who get to have their fun. Meanwhile they tell me how they hope their wives haven't done anything while they've been gone. It sounds hypocritical to me. A woman has as much right for sexual pleasure as men. They're hungry for it too. Sometimes, one man just simply isn't enough. Men take on other women anyway, so why is it that women should feel shame?"

Andrew slapped her.

Miyako looked at him feeling the fox fire up in her eyes. Perhaps the spirit of the Kitsune was within her all along, or perhaps she somehow merged with it now. Miyako slapped him back with the comb, breaking it in the process, and allowed it to drop on the floor. Then she turned to leave.

He sighed. He asked her to wait. Miyako froze, but didn't turn around.

"Perhaps you're right. Maybe it isn't fair to think like that. Maybe we should all keep everything in our pants."

"Is that really possible? I doubt a man is truly capable of forgoing sex without going crazy. Certainly, a lot of men would go insane if no woman was willing to be with them. Or the man would just take what he wanted. So what choice do women have? Or at least all of us? Only some of us would be marriage material otherwise. While some of us are doomed to be these prostitutes, things you called us. But men can do whatever? What's to say a woman wants to be with a man like that? A man who had his way with various women, while she remains sexually starved to stay pure for him? But you know women take it anyway. They choose to ignore it. So why should you be so harsh? Sex is such a beautiful thing. It isn't something to be wasted. All of our sexual desires and experiences are valid."

Miyako took a few more steps toward the door but froze again. She added one last thought.

"I don't understand your judgment. You used me sexually too and you've loved it the whole time. You loved using my body as you pleased and used me as a stand-in lover. Maybe that word is really a good thing after all. Prostitute. I take no shame in it. Perhaps you're the one who does because you fear your own sexuality or seeing hunger in women, you can't fulfill. You were far from being my greatest lover. It'd be wise to look at that before blaming a woman for wanting other men."

Miyako's took off the ring and threw it at him. Then she slammed the door behind her.

***

She went home. Along the way, she spied foxes watching her. She was pleased. She knew she'd freed herself from a terrible future. She prided herself in finally being able to stand up for herself, even to an American. She reached her apartment. When she opened the door, she immediately jumped into her bed. She was glad to feel warm and safe. Relief washed over her. It was over. She didn't even feel bad about offending an American hero.

Although, he proved not to be much of a hero after all. What war hero slaps a woman he loves? She hoped he wouldn't be so terrible to his wife. Or not marry at all. She pitied all of his future lovers. No wonder Lily turned him down. Miyako would have liked the girl. She too was strong enough to say no to him. They could have gossiped about Andrew over wine and chocolate. Too bad they would probably never meet. They were worlds apart, not just geographically either. Oceans wouldn't be their only barrier in relation.

Miyako wasn't even mad she was missing out on what might have been her only chance to have sex that day. True masturbation wasn't as good as sex, but it was a worthy substitute in cases like this. She could imagine herself with her favorite lovers, even her dream soldier. Play it guilt free in her mind as she ravaged herself to climax. When she finished, she chowed down on boxed chocolates a lover left for her, chasing it with wine left by another.

This was way better than anything Andrew was bound to offer her. Miyako knew she was never going to see him again. She was content with that. She was still in shock, an American soldier, the perfect hero, had failed her in this way. These men were supposed to be perfect. These were her protectors. Her means of livelihood. Her lovers. They defeated the Japanese men after all, and were rebuilding her country for the better. That was their plan anyway. She became independent because of them.

But another thought now troubled Miyako. She remembered the man she'd beaten in the street. The Japanese man. The only Japanese man she had a conversation with since taking her train ride years ago. He said she wasn't independent at all but a tool to the Americans. She hadn't believed him at the time, assuming he just felt emasculated by her work. Now she was seeing there was truth to what he said after all.

In a way, she'd become dependent on the Americans. It wasn't just because of the money they paid her or the sexual acts they exchanged. It went deeper than that. She valued them above herself. She tried to discard everything Japanese in order to follow the American way. She'd used them to forget the pains of her past by enslaving herself to the American dream. Enslaving herself to the pleasures of men, and her own pleasure as well. She built a new cage for herself after she'd escape her old one.

Was that all life was? A series of cages? Was there a way to escape?

Miyako didn't want to live in a cage. She wanted true freedom. But did such a thing exist? Was America's motto of liberty a lie? Was anyone truly free?

Yet, Miyako never felt alive until she started romancing the Americans. Having sex with men of war, receiving gifts, all the new delicious food, the romance, the money. All of it was so intoxicating. Even if she knew it couldn't last.

Perhaps people became comfortable in their cages and felt there was no pleasure in the world outside. Miyako was content in hers for years before this point.

Now she wanted something else.

Marriage would be a change at least. A chance at a new life. Roger could lead her in this new chapter just as Shinju had in the old one. She could even get a new kind of job. The thought made Miyako laugh. Perhaps she could be a housewife and mother. Perhaps this new life could last so much longer than her current one, only ending in happiness and bliss, death and contentment in old age. Miyako liked the thought of that.

Yet, as the days went on, her vision of marrying Roger became bleaker. Her fantasies of that life took on a grayness with no vibrancy. Shouldn't this be her chance at a happy ending? Going to America with a man she loved and escaping her past permanently? At least the parts of Japan she wanted to leave behind. Miyako kept adorning herself with Roger's pink stone only to take it off again. Not just when she was out in public, she felt shame wearing it when she was alone too. She couldn't decide if she wanted to see the ring on her finger or not. It was so beautiful and Miyako wanted to keep it. The ring still reminded her of the cherry blossoms. At the same time, she didn't want to do what she needed to in return for wearing it. The obligation it represented. The weight of a promise to one man. A hefty price for such a small and pretty thing.

***

Miyako pondered her doubts on her upcoming marriage without discovering a solution she could feel at peace with. She was trying to wrap things up with her clients, but she still didn't have the heart to tell them she was getting married. Instead, she kept going through the motions, fully aware Roger would now consider this cheating. He wanted a monogamous relationship with her for the rest of their lives. He'd made that clear in their last conversation.

Miyako was so scared of losing him that she actually considered marriage as a way to keep such a wonderful man forever. But she didn't want to lose out on the other men either. That scared her too. She wasn't sure which prospect she was more terrified with.

Instead of going celibate before marriage, Miyako only slowed down with the other men temporarily until she started having more sex with them than ever. She fucked her clients over and over again at night, until they told her to stop from pure exhaustion. Miyako was sneaking out of hotels at night after fucking one client to go find another one to fuck. She was finding more new clients than ever. She was having sex with two or three different men a night, sometimes more. One night it was six men, another night Miyako lost count.

Sometimes she didn't feel anything during intercourse at all. Her mind traveled somewhere even she couldn't recall. She'd look up and suddenly it would all be over and she would move onto the next man. Miyako used sex as a form of maintenance, her body a machine that would stop running if she took too long between partners. She was running away from something in herself and sex was the only distraction. The only thing she felt comfortable doing. All she felt she had left. Yet, her body was wearing down from it all.

Miyako sought any military men, even the kinds she previously avoided. There was no more note-taking. No more studying the desires of her men. No more romance. Just action fueled by pure sexual fury and lust. She asked to be punished, beaten, maimed. Secretly, she hoped the men would destroy her.

She asked for weapons of war to be used on her. With each act, Miyako pleaded to go further.

There were knives, etching battles and writing, the pain lingered. Fists changing the color of her skin. A gun she made love to which was loaded. Grenades she rubbed herself upon. Bullets she consumed to prove her servitude. Damage she committed on herself without prompt or request. Her men weren't willing to hurt her like she wanted to be. After the gunfire and bombs, did they have nothing left for her? They were haunted by emotions from the war, yet couldn't release them upon her.

She found new men who would.

She wondered when Roger would notice her self-destruction. How she would explain herself on their wedding night with her naked body painted in red, white, and blue. If that night would even come.

Her new men punished and humiliated her. They watched her fuck other women only to join in when they found fit. Miyako barely noticed the women at all, they were phantoms to her, nearly nonexistent except for their sexual purpose. She ignored them other than that, looking more at their breasts and lips while avoiding their eyes entirely. She cared not for them or their pleasure, the men's pleasure, or her own. Miyako was shocked and sickened by all of the things that could cause her to orgasm. How a gun, a woman's cry, and pain could set her off. How the aftermath of war all set her to that ultimate climax. Miyako was terrified. Yet, she refused to stop.

War hadn't killed her before. All these years later, Miyako pushed to become just another casualty to its aftermath.

***

Miyako agreed to a threesome with two new men she met at the movies. She knew Roger would have been furious. He'd express distaste for women who allowed two guys to take her at once. He felt it showed a lack of self-respect. That's why she did it. Miyako knew Roger hadn't told her the whole story behind his revulsion to such activity. She knew a woman he loved must have hurt him this way. Committing this act would hit a weak nerve, causing him to relive a painful memory. Perhaps it would get him to leave her. But would it make him unable to love again? Miyako didn't want to punish him just for loving her. She debated returning his ring as she had Andrew's. Roger was a better man than Andrew. A better person than her. His true happily ever after was across the ocean within the arms of another.

Yet, these two men wanted her in a way she dared not refuse. Their desire reminded her of the excitement she felt when she first started her line of work. Infatuation forced her to orgasm several times in quick succession.

Feeling two men inside of her at once made her feel as if she would burst out of her skin, escaping all the pain and confines of her world. Of politics and war. Of America and Japan. Of men and women. Life and death.

Sex was always a way out of it all. A way to forget and delay. Yet a method to reach the deepest beauty of what life could offer. She wanted to experience it all while she still had the chance. Before she told Roger and ruined everything. Or before she married him with so many new secrets, Miyako wouldn't even begin to know how to hide them all. Which ones she would even still remember.

One of the men felt like a normal man, acting on physical pleasure and instinct. The other was different. He vibrated with another energy entirely. He was filling her with his energy. She felt white light moving within her, reaching her darkest parts. This made Miyako orgasm more and more, but in the beautiful and pure way she hadn't experienced through sex before. The other man left, too exhausted to keep going. He left money next to the bed and walked out. Miyako barely noticed. This other man was filling her, satisfying her. Making her feel love again. Reminding her what she believed and who she was. It felt like days went by as they stayed like this, powerful love traveling between two of them. She was sharing something beautiful again. But it was beyond what she experienced before. This is how she wanted her life to be.

Afterward the man lingered with her, cuddling her in bed and stroking her cheek. He told her he wished he could bring her home. He would love to have a girl like her. He still was vibrating. Miyako could still feel the light inside of his heart.

It took everything Miyako had left not to cry. At least he didn't pull out a ring on her, she thought to herself. But then he stroked her naked ring finger, as if reading her thoughts. She could bare it no longer. Miyako wept rivers of tears. Tornados of sounds emulated from her mouth. She shook like an earthquake. Her body was its own instrument of sorrow, opened and exposed. He asked her what was wrong, if he'd hurt her in some way. She told him no. She just didn't want to ever get married. The man told her she never had to. This was her life, and she could do what she wanted. Miyako took comfort in that. He was filling her with light again even though he wasn't inside her any longer. She felt peace for the first time since all of this began.

She agreed to meet with him again, but alone this time. Even though she didn't even remember his name. She wasn't even fully sure what he looked liked. She had joined him sexually in the swirl she had with the other men as of late, but he was something more entirely.

***

Miyako started to wonder if she could stop having sex with other men. Every encounter made her realize more and more that she didn't want her current lifestyle to end. She didn't want to lose out on that high feeling which came with new lovers. At the same time, attaining that feeling was now all-consuming. Sex with men was all she could think of. Everything she did was a ritual to prepare for that end. Without any joy or satisfaction beyond the physical release, which felt less genuine with each encounter.

It was as if all of her sexual escapades were in fast-forward, she could barely live through and remember them. Miyako let herself become a sexual object instead, going through the motions of giving herself to a man to orgasm again and again

Her vagina was so sore, and she was beginning to close. Men were finding it harder to make their way inside. She didn't know how to let them in. She was having so many orgasms per day it was becoming difficult to orgasm with the last men of the night. Soon all she was doing was providing a warm body to be fondled and fucked, too exhausted for enthusiasm and mutual rhythm. She kept telling herself the men wouldn't notice, but she felt in their bodies they indeed had. She was too broken to provide for her original use. They didn't see her the same way. She didn't see them or herself the same way either. Underneath her dark circles, chipped nail polish, and blotchy skin was a lost woman she didn't know.

Wearing herself out made her face another reality. Miyako would get old someday. The day would come when she would be too old to have sex, too old to take on new lovers, too old to be beautiful. Men wouldn't want her anymore. What then? Roger would be there. To love her wrinkles and her graying hair. He would always remember how she looked when she was young. But he would still find her beautiful when she was old. He told her all of this while they'd been among the cherry blossoms.

Why did she doubt her future with him? Why couldn't she be faithful to his promise?

***

Miyako was lost in her thoughts no matter where she was in her physical world. Whether walking, eating, fucking, or sleeping. Her dream soldier always lingering in the back of her mind, no matter how hard she tried to push him away. She longed for his existence. She still masturbated to him when she was alone at night. She preferred this to sex now.

But Roger was real, and this man might not be. Even if he was, it's likely he wouldn't want her. He could be so in love with war, he may not have room to love her. Even though she herself was a product of war. She would have wasted a perfectly good marriage. Unless the marriage wasn't perfectly good after all. Was that possible despite Roger being so good?

***

Miyako visited the grave of Shinju's sunglasses. She prayed to her and hoped she could help her, one last time. But loud Shinju was silent in death. After waiting in a kneeling position in front of the grave, Miyako's cluttered mind made room to once again pity Shinju. Perhaps Shinju needed silence more than Miyako needed answers. After all, Shinju suffered more deeply in life than Miyako ever would. She needed peace now, and Miyako felt guilty for trying to disturb her.

As she left the graveyard, a fox peered at her from behind the trees. Whenever she went for the rest of the day, she'd seen it peeking out from a distance too far for her to catch the fox before it disappeared again. She felt its eyes watching her even as she laid herself down to sleep that night.

***

Miyako met with the mysterious man again, whose name she finally remembered was Todd, the one who somehow filled her with light. No blue lipstick this time. She didn't need it for him. Over burgers and milkshakes, they talked about America and Japan. But he seemed more interested in her story than anything else. At first, Miyako resisted telling him anything. He'd already seen so much of her. She was scared to show more.

Todd coaxed her gently with persistence and warmth. Soon Miyako caved and admitted to it all. Her lonely childhood which made her all the more willing to leave behind her family, her culture, and her country. Meeting Shinju. Embarking all kind of sexual escapades. Having power, money, and freedom for the first time. Rebelling against the confines of her old life and believing Americans were the solution to all her old sorrows.

Drew's suicide. The decline of her friend, the mystery behind it, and the few answers which came.

Shinju's death. Discovering the Americans weren't perfect. She was so angry at herself now for not seeing them sooner. They were only men after all.

Then the two marriage proposals. The rejection of one and the hesitation of the other. Her recent self-destruction.

Binding it all was the war. What it destroyed. What Miyako was able to create in its wake. Yet, it maintained a haunting presence over everything around her. Her home, her men, her dreams, her life. She wasn't sure how to feel about it all.

Miyako trusted Todd entirely with her whole life. She wasn't sure why. She felt safer with him than with anyone, including Roger. It was as if he'd been there all along from her birth and watched her whole life unfold. Knowing every detail by heart and was just happy Miyako was revealing all of her truth. This was a confession not to him, but to herself. Miyako felt this to be true, despite her logic telling her it wasn't possible. He was just a man after all. When there were no more words to say, Todd smiled. He held her hand and looked deep into her eyes. Miyako finally noticed his eyes weren't that of a man.

They were fox eyes. Was this the same Kitsune spirit she'd seen following her? The one who appeared before her previously as a man? Had followed her out of the graveyard? Who appeared to her again and again? Or was he one of many she'd seen?

Todd dissolved into a fox right before her eyes. It happened as quickly and seamlessly as the fall of rain or the rising sun. He ran off in broad daylight only looking back at her once when he reached the edge of the woods. Then he disappeared into the trees. The people at the restaurant and walking nearby continued with their own business. Miyako was speechless. She was the only one aware it happened at all.

Of all things she'd done, had she also fucked a fox spirit?

Was it from the alcohol? She didn't drink like Shinju or her clients. Was her lack of sleep causing her to hallucinate? Or was it real? Had she'd been blessed by the Kitsunes?

Miyako pulled her the bottle of Tabasco sauce from her purse. She poured a lake of hot sauce onto her burger and ate it to keep herself set in reality. The heat and spice seemed to help. But then she realized she absentmindedly added a few drops to her ice cream shake. She didn't even remembering ordering it in the first place.

Staring at the swirl of vanilla and chocolate that would never be pure again, it hit her. She wasn't going to marry Roger. She didn't love him.

She liked him, loved him a certain way, but she wasn't in love with him. She loved him enough to give her body to him and please him. But she didn't love him enough to give her life to him. That was the difference. She hadn't loved her other clients either. She'd been lumping all the different kinds of romantic feelings together, even though, her own fantasies showed her there was a deeper love out there still. One she hadn't experienced yet, but could commit herself to.

There was no reason to feel guilt over her dream soldier. She didn't have enough love for the man who gave her the beautiful ring even if it did remind her of cherry blossoms. Even if Roger was an amazing man.

She craved the emotional depths. Deeper than anything she felt for any of her clients. She dreamed of that other man because she knew that ability for deeper love was in her. Love of this kind was something she truly wanted. Love, which went beyond the depths of sex. The Americans expanded her awareness of the depths relationships could take. Now she would seek to go beyond this. Americans couldn't show her the rest of the way. She would have to find it herself.

Miyako knew she'd rather search for that love rather than settle on someone else. Her dream soldier. It didn't matter if she was never pleasured by this man. All that mattered was chasing the possibility of finding him. The journey would cause her to go beyond anything this life offered her so far. Her life would be a dream whether he existed or not. He was something to aspire toward. Not just because of the prospect of finding him, but in what she had to become in order to be with him. She knew she would have to find herself beyond what she could provide for a man. She needed to be strong, truly independent, not just in the forms within her current lifestyle. Be able to survive and thrive no matter what was thrown at her. She'd survived the war after all. This time she would be able to adapt while always being herself. The search and journey for him would be worth it regardless if she found him or not.

The kind of man she sought couldn't take a woman who would slow him down from his mission. One that went beyond the power struggles of politics and war. He would serve something greater.

Miyako would need her own mission too. But what would it be? Before she dedicated herself to pleasure and romance. Now she wanted to dedicate her life to true love, pure and whole. Could she teach others to love one another? Or would she dedicate herself to something else. She needed to make her life full, and this was how to do it. It wasn't just about being worthy of her dream man, but about being worthy of living this life. Now that she owned her freedom, she wanted to find something worth serving instead of being a slave to primal desires. That would be how she would finally become free.

If this man existed, she would find him. Otherwise, she would be content being in love with the idea of him and what it inspired in her own life. She would always feel him with her in her dreams and waking life. She could make love to his presence even without using her physical body. The idea of him owned her heart. She couldn't marry another when she was already so in love with this dream. Regardless of the circumstances. Regardless of reality versus dreams; the world which lay before her and the possibilities of another.

***

Miyako knew she couldn't stay in Japan, or Roger would find her. He wanted to save her. But Miyako knew she couldn't count on him or any other man, American or not, to save her. She needed to save herself as she did years ago. She needed to break the mold of her life again as she did once before. She couldn't continue her lifestyle of romance any longer. She would stay celibate for a while. Find new ways to fill herself. Sex would take on a new meaning, one she would discover in time.

The wedding was only a few weeks away. She was still meeting with Roger to make plans for the future. She did this with the sinking knowledge of her past betrayals as well as the ultimate one to come. He'd asked her about children and if she'd be okay with a dog. Assured her she wouldn't have to work ever again. He hoped she'd learn how to cook but he promised he could cook a mean stew. He would be happy to finally feed her the recipes passed down to him from generations of grandfathers and grandmothers past. He would be so happy to have her meet what family he had, and to give her a family as well. He wanted to mend and heal the trouble she'd dealt within her own family. He expected his home to be spotlessly clean. He offered to help her with that though since he was a neat freak himself. But he stressed he didn't want to pressure her either. He didn't want to trap her into being a perfect housewife. Miyako feared otherwise.

Roger asked her if she was into gardening. He thought they could have a rose garden just for her, and could find other flowers to grow too. He told her his hometown of Philadelphia even had cherry blossoms. There were other places in America they could go to see them such as New York City and the nation's capital Washington DC. They could explore the United States together. He spoke of road trips and exotic vacations. Of what kind of kids they'd have and which of Miyako's traits he hoped they'd inherited, like her eyes and hair. She could even join a women's club to make friends. He would teach her how to fish if she wanted. He'd even teach her how to shoot to defend herself when he wasn't home. She could take any kind of music classes she wanted. She could pick the curtains, wallpaper, carpet, and bedding in their new home. They'd grow old together. Have their happily ever after. It would all be so perfect.

Most of his monologue warmed her heart. He'd spent so long thinking this through. Pieces of her loved the life he painted for them. He wanted to build something beautiful with her. Miyako would imagine herself doing the things he described, and for a few moments, she would almost be willing to fall under the spell of his dreams. Her mind told her to do so. Say yes to the marriage. Yes to America. Yes to this new life.

But deep down Miyako felt sick. Her heart wasn't with him anymore. Marriage, a house, a family all seemed to be an invitation, another cage. She never told Roger this. She wanted him to believe she was still excited.

She didn't want to cause such pain to a man she felt so much for. She feared she was making the same mistake with Roger she'd made with Andrew by avoiding telling the truth because of the hurt it would bring. Except this time, she didn't think she'd have the strength to do the right thing. She cared for Roger deeply and hurting him would hurt her more than it would with any other man she'd known. He was her first, not just sexually but romantically too. He was still her greatest love. Even if that love wasn't true.

She couldn't find the right words to tell him all she wanted to. She loved him but didn't love him at the same time. She couldn't marry him. She loved another who may or may not exist. Roger could never have her full heart. That she needed to take another journey instead though she didn't know where she was going. He deserved a wife who loved him fully. He deserved a future she couldn't give him.

She knew him well enough to know he wouldn't understand. To know what he'd say. He would tell her she was having cold feet, scared to move away from her homeland. Scared he would leave her alone in America. He'd say she loved him and he loved her, and love was a scary thing at times. But it was worth the leap. He would promise to take care of her and make everything right. He'd promised it would all be great. Their happily ever after

At that point, Miyako would either have to run away, which he'd likely catch her or she would simply go with him to America and suffer in her silence as Roger thought all was right. She decided she wouldn't tell him anything at all. She would leave Japan before she left Roger at the altar.

At least then, she wouldn't have to see his face when he learned they wouldn't be married. She didn't think she could bear the heartbreak.

Miyako left her ring behind in her apartment. Perhaps Roger would find it there, among the rest of her things. She thought about leaving a note, but in the end, she couldn't imagine the little English writing she knew would suffice for anything. He would understand that less than any words she could say. She cleaned her room before leaving the key in her bed. She slipped the ring onto the key, and placed it on her pillow leaving one final blue kiss near it, she was leaving the rest of her lipstick behind as well, so it would be easy to find. Or perhaps he wouldn't. He might not be able to find it among what she was leaving behind. The soldiers' gifts and most of her clothes. Her stuffed animals. The jewelry box he crafted himself. She'd locked herself out. Unless Roger got the landlord to let him in, he wouldn't be able to find it. She would have left her door unlocked to make it easier for him, but she didn't want to risk any temptation to return.

***

As Miyako did all those years ago, she got on the train with no idea where she was heading. Except this time, she was filled with hope. She would have a tomorrow. One of her own making. She wouldn't just fall into something that had been presented to her. Her entire life would be intentional, focused on love and something greater. She would find something in which she could create meaning in the world. Make it grow, make it last.

During her last trip on the train, the spirits had been with her. They'd always been with her, even though she didn't know this at the time. They'd taken the forms of men and foxes. Perhaps those forms suited her best, or perhaps she could just simply see these kinds of spirits. It didn't matter. Like an owl that flew and disappeared into the trees, spirits watched from the darkness. Invisible but powerfully real. Pulling strings and whispering in the dark, the spirits would be with her as mirrors to discover her inner depth in the dark. They would be with her as she moved forward.

Miyako wondered what would become of Japan, if it would weave in and out of its own culture as well as American culture. To Miyako, America breathed new life into her country and into her. Just a few years ago Japan was a ghost land, a shadow of its former self. Miyako was too. Brought back from the brink of death, she was not only granted new life but freedom. Freedom beyond anything she could ever imagined. A freedom the men of her country would have never allowed. Would Japan fall back into old patterns of not letting the women be free? The woman would have to take it by force instead. They would find their own way in time.

Perhaps things would be even better as Japan found itself again in a form it could proudly flourish in. Where both men and women were free to find beauty and pleasure. It wasn't about rejecting the past, but learning how to create a new future despite it. A future that honored a better life for everyone.

Miyako found herself not by becoming more American, but being released from her past so she could find herself. Yet, Miyako looked to her own future now. Where she wanted to go, who she wanted to be. The Americans couldn't tell her that. Only she could. She owned herself and her life. That's all that mattered.

Miyako remembered when her mother told her she would always need a man; a woman couldn't survive in the world on her own even though a man could. She would never escape men and their power over her. These are ideas Miyako's mother tried to force upon her.

Miyako laughed despite the painful memories. What horrible rules ruled her mother and sister. She was saddened by this but found solace in escaping herself. Perhaps she could live for them too. Live for the freedom they never found the courage to seek for themselves. She would appreciate her own freedom that much more.

Miyako learned to take care of herself in spite what her mother said. At the same time, she proved her mother right in needing men, but they weren't husbands or family her mother spoke of. Miyako still needed men, but she needed herself more than anyone else. She could never fully escape men, nor did she want to. Men could be a source of pain or pleasure, often both. Miyako knew it was the same for women as well. Everyone contained their own sorrows, their own power.

She watched Mount Fuji from her window. The mountain withstood change with quiet acceptance and grace. What had it seen? What did it see now? What would it witness as the times moved forward? How did Japan look from that mountaintop? Miyako would have loved to know. Climb up and see for herself.

She could do anything she wanted, she was fully capable.

Though she knew, she couldn't return for a long time.

Miyako saw foxes running through the forest. They played and danced like the wild animals they were. A few joined them who seemed to be creatures beyond this earth. Kitsumes, Miyako knew. Blending together so no one could tell the difference between them.

The spirits meshed perfectly with the human world so well they weren't always noticed. Yet, they were always in harmony. Miyako could see that from her train window. They were outside the prisons of the human world.

She'd ride the current of her heart. Act on instinct as the foxes did. This way Miyako could live a life of pleasure and beauty. Just as nature intended.

Amaterasu emerged from the cave and the sun returned. Light radiated upon her people as she returned to her rightful place in the sky.

Historical Note

Viewing the Pan Pan simply as prostitutes or sexual tools provides no justice to their movement as a subculture as well as to their individual identities. It misses their unique influence that extends beyond Japan, despite only being active for the first few years after the war. While they were controversial figures, they remain important ones.

They symbolized survival after WWII. Women who no longer had men to support them due to the war, now found a way to support themselves. Often they ended up making more money than their husbands and fathers ever had.

They represented liberation after breaking free of an overly militarized government. They defied cultural norms in order to freely express what authority worked to previously silence. They partook in PDA. They were forthcoming with their sexual intent and desires. They cursed aloud.

They rejected their own culture and Americanized themselves. Taking fashion brought along with the United States military and civilians, they developed a style that took on a life of its own. Certain fashion trends thriving in Japan are attributed to the Pan Pans.

They were free to pick clients based on their preference. Most only catered to American GIs. Some took only black clients. Through their openness with clientele, they transcended racial divides.

They were free of pimps and brothels. Yet, there were still the dangers that came with the lifestyle. There were issues of turf and dealing with territorial women. Dangers of rape, STDs, and murder.

American GIs were caught off guard but generally delighted by the Pan Pans' openness in language and sexuality. But others felt threatened by them. Japanese men felt emasculated by the Pan Pan. The Japanese government was horrified they existed. Feminist frowned upon them. Police aided in their removal. However, many of their reports gave us what little information we have about them today.

Consumerization of sex still echoes on. This is not only the case in Japan, where sex is the second leading industry in the economy, but in many parts of the world. On a deeper level, the desire of women wanting more, not only in terms of sex, but in the ways of romance remains just as relevant not only in Japan but across the globe.

Despite this, the Pan Pan have been forgotten.

Until now.

Bibliography

Dower, John W. Embracing Defeat: Japan in the Wake of World War II. New York: WW Norton & Company, 1999.

Gate of Flesh (Nikutai no mon). dir. Seijun Suzuki. perf. Yumiko Nogawa. Nikkatsu, 1964.

Georgie Andrews. Personal Interview. June, July and August 2011.

Mark James McLelland. "Kissing Is a Symbol of Democracy! Dating, Democracy and Romance in Occupied Japan 1945-1952." Faculty of Arts - Papers (2010) http://works.bepress.com/mmclelland/10 (Accessed June 1st, 2011)

Mastsuma Goya. Personal Interview. December 2011.

Moslasky, Micheal S. The American Occupation of Japan and Okinawa; Literature and Memory. Routledge: London 1999.

Narumi, Hiroshi, and Valerie Steele, and Patricia Mears, and Yuiya Kawamura. Japan Fashion Now. New Haven and London: Yale University Press, 2010.

Sanders, Holly Vincele. Prostitution in Postwar Japan: Debt and Labor. Princeton University, 2005.

About Paige Ethridge

A voice has been inside Paige since she was young to write stories. She graduated from SUNY Purchase's highly selective Lily Lieb Port Writing Program with a dual degree in history and creative writing. She freelanced for several publications, including *Inked Magazine,* mostly writing about MMA and alternative culture. She's a black belt in Shaolin Kempo Karate, a Pisces sun with a Leo moon, and avid cook. She lives with her husband Scott and dog Athena near Virginia Beach.

Social Media

Instagram: https://www.instagram.com/paige.etheridge/

LinkedIn: https://www.linkedin.com/in/paige-etheridge-21370b46

Twitter: https://twitter.com/PaigeEtheridge1

Acknowledgements

Brett Kaplan, thank you so much for being with me from my first revision of this project. Scott Schneider, for being a supportive husband and nurturer of all my dreams. Terri Roughton, for force feeding me literature from a young age and ensuring I had the best in my English education. To my beta readers, Rebecca Rose Downs, Laura Gravatt, Sara Roncero-Menendez, and Candy Wallace. To Ian Johnson and Deidra Catero for their loving support. To Matsuma Goya and Georgie Andrews for giving me a deep view on what Japan was really like during the time of this story.